LISTEN

Praise for Kris Bryant

Against All Odds

"This story tugged at my heartstrings, and it hit all the right notes for me because these wonderful authors allowed me to peep into the hearts and minds of the characters. The vivid descriptions of Peyton, Tory, and the perpetrator's personalities allowed me to have a deeper understanding of what makes them tick, and I was able to form a clear picture of them in my mind."—*The Lesbian Review*

"*Against All Odds* is equal parts thriller and romance; the balance between action and love, fast and slow pace makes this novel a very entertaining read."—*Lez Review Books*

Lammy Finalist *Jolt*

Jolt "is a magnificent love story. Two women hurt by their previous lovers and each in their own way trying to make sense out of life and times. When they meet at a gay- and lesbian-friendly summer camp, they both feel as if lightning has struck. This is so beautifully involving, I have already reread it twice. Amazing!"—*Rainbow Book Reviews*

Breakthrough

"Looking for a fun and funny light read with hella cute animal antics and a smoking hot butch ranger? Look no further... In this well-written first-person narrative, Kris Bryant's characters are well developed, and their push/pull romance hits all the right beats, making it a delightful read just in time for beach reading."—*Writing While Distracted*

"[A]n exceptional book that has a few twists and turns that catch you out and make you wish the book would never end. I was captivated from the beginning and can't wait to see how Bryant will top this."—*Les Rêveur*

"It's hilariously funny, romantic, and oh so sexy…But it is the romance between Kennedy and Brynn that stole my heart. The passion and emotion in the love scenes surpassed anything Kris Bryant has written before. I loved it."—*Kitty Kat's Book Review Blog*

"Kris Bryant has written several enjoyable contemporary romances, and *Breakthrough* is no exception. It's interesting and clearly well-researched, giving us information about Alaska and issues like poaching and conservation in a way that's engaging and never comes across as an info dump. She also delivers her best character work to date, going deeper with Kennedy and Brynn than we've seen in previous stories. If you're a fan of Kris Bryant, you won't want to miss this book, and if you're a fan of romance in general, you'll want to pick it up, too."—*Lambda Literary*

Forget Me Not

"Told in the first person, from Grace's point of view, we are privy to Grace's inner musings and her vulnerabilities… Bryant crafts clever wording to infuse Grace with a sharp-witted personality, which clearly covers her insecurities… This story is filled with loving familial interactions, caring friends, romantic interludes, and tantalizing sex scenes. The dialogue, both among the characters and within Grace's head, is refreshing, original, and sometimes comical. *Forget Me Not* is a fresh perspective on a romantic theme, and an entertaining read."—*Lambda Literary Review*

Forget Me Not

Kris Bryant "has a way of giving insight into the other main protagonist by using a few clever techniques and involving the secondary characters to add back-stories and extra pieces of important information. The pace of the book was excellent, it was never rushed but I was never bored or waiting for a chapter to finish...this epilogue made my heart swell to the point I almost lunged off the sofa to do a happy dance."
—*Les Rêveur*

"[I]t just hits the right note all the way...[A] very good read if you are looking for a sweet romance."—*Lez Review Books*

Whirlwind Romance

"Ms. Bryant's descriptions were written with such passion and colorful detail that you could feel the tension and the excitement along with the characters."—*Inked Rainbow Reviews*

Taste

"*Taste* is a student/teacher romance set in a culinary school. If the premise makes you wonder whether this book will make you want to eat something tasty, the answer is: yes."
—*The Lesbian Review*

Touch

"The sexual chemistry in this book is off the hook. Kris Bryant writes my favorite sex scenes in lesbian romantic fiction."
—*Les Rêveur*

LISTEN

by

Kris Bryant

2019

LISTEN

ISBN 13: 978-1-63555-318-5

This Trade Paperback Original Is Published By
Bold Strokes Books, Inc.
P.O. Box 249
Valley Falls, NY 12185

First Edition: February 2019

CREDITS
EDITOR: ASHLEY TILLMAN
PRODUCTION DESIGN: STACIA SEAMAN
COVER CONCEPT BY DEB B.
COVER DESIGN BY SHERI (HINDSIGHTGRAPHICS@GMAIL.COM) AND KRIS BRYANT

Acknowledgments

Always and forever, a big thank you to Radclyffe and Sandy for giving me the go-ahead on my books. I love being a part of the Bold Strokes Books family, I really do.

Thank you, Ashley, for talking me through the rough stuff and ensuring that my words flow and tell the story the way I meant to, not the way I actually wrote it.

A heartfelt thank you to Deb for reviewing the music and descriptions in this book. I can't read music, and sometimes the words fail me when I'm trying to describe something. Thank you for your patience in figuring out what I was saying and helping me through this process. Also, I wanted a simple and strong cover, and you came up with exactly what I wanted in thirty seconds. You're fantastic and I couldn't have done this without you.

When we are little, we dream big. I always wanted to be a writer. A lot of people wanted to be rock stars or play in symphonies. Most of my friends were in band or took private music lessons, and I was always curious who would make it big. Here's to all of those young musicians who wanted to be up on stage, but somehow, life headed them down a different path. Music touches all of us. It lifts us up, it brings us down, it fills us with great joy and affects many of us deeper than almost anything else. Music helps me survive. It calms me faster than any other exercise I can do to handle my anxiety. I count it, I tap to it, I even lose myself in the meaning of the words. I hope everyone who suffers with anxiety has a coping mechanism that is as perfect for them as music is for me.

This book is dedicated to everyone
who suffers from and soldiers through anxiety.
You aren't alone and you should never feel that way.

CHAPTER ONE

The nightmares followed me everywhere and never faded in intensity. Thirteen years going strong and still a surprise. I would go months without a single dream and the minute anything in my routine changed, bam. A visit from my past. Last night's was horrific. I was back onstage at the Kimmel Center for the Performing Arts in front of a sold-out crowd of thousands dressed in their finery. I wore a black velvet dress that brushed past my knees and clung to my thin waist with a white sash that tied in back. My hair was styled up and made me seem older than fourteen. My velvet flats matched my dress and were soundless when I walked out to welcoming applause. For most musicians, that was the sound of success. For me, it was my ultimate terror. I knew I would fail before I placed a single finger on the perfectly weighted keys. I couldn't move. I felt a resounding shift take place in my brain as my whole life changed. I shattered inside. Every single part of me broke that day.

My ill-timed nightmare pushed me out of sleep I desperately needed. I looked at the clock. Three fifteen. I stared up at the ceiling and knew my shot at falling back to sleep was gone. I should just get the day started. Clio jumped up on the bed and meowed at me. I knew he felt my anxiety. For an alley cat with a chewed-up ear and a limp, he was great at reading my moods. When he found me two years ago, he looked like I felt most days—beat up and dragging through life. I couldn't help but bond with him. We were soul mates. We understood each other. I stroked his soft fur and felt his sweet purrs rumble against my chest. It calmed me.

"What do you think, buddy? Too early to get going? Will I look like a freak if I show up two hours early?" I nodded. I swore he nodded back. "Let's at least get up and eat something. I'll have coffee and you can have milk."

Clio had a stomach of steel after a life out on the streets. He could and would eat anything. Milk did not bother him. He preferred Baileys, but I figured that danced on the borderline of animal abuse, so he was only allowed a lick of it on holidays. I poured him a saucer of two percent and placed it next to his untouched kibble. He liked it when I added wet food to the dry. I grabbed a can and scraped the contents into his bowl.

"My turn." I decided on oatmeal and a cup of coffee. Today was a big day. I'd been assigned a two-month project with a sister company of ours on the other side of town. I normally worked from home four days a week. The fifth day was in the office of Banks Corporation, and it was always a struggle for me to be social. Starting today, though, I was to analyze data for the next eight weeks with people I didn't know. The extra incentive pay was fantastic, but I communicated better with plants and animals. That was why my job was perfect. Plus, I got to watch *Jeopardy* in my pajamas and do math problems during commercials. I was living my ideal life. Or at least the life I chose for myself.

"Should I wear the gray or the black suit?" My eyes traveled over both, back and forth, until they landed and stayed on the black. Clio yawned at my choice. I looked at him. "I'll wear the blue blouse with it." The blue was a good choice because it was the same color as my eyes. Dark, sapphire blue. I jumped in the shower, washed my hair, and carefully styled it. Even procrastinating as much as I had, I was still going to be early. I figured I could at least check out the area and find the best places for lunch and coffee. An insurance company with the entire loft of a building in Lincoln Park was going to have a lot of options. And a lot of people.

I piled on the antiperspirant and prayed I wouldn't sweat through my blouse, or worse, my suit jacket. Five forty-five. I could catch the early train in and be there by seven. That would give me time to get my bearings, figure out where I needed to be, and find Darren Hoyt, my point of contact for the project. I pictured a sixty-year-old man with wisps of graying hair poking out of a shiny balding head, and a mustache that hung too far over his lip. Glasses, too. Readers that he constantly searched for before finding them tucked in his shirt pocket or perched on his forehead. My imagination was getting the best of me. Submerging myself in people again was probably the best thing for me. It had been a while. "Behave, Clio. Don't tell me the final *Jeopardy* answer." I kissed his nose and left my apartment.

The L station was two blocks away. I had to slow my steps because I felt I was nearly jogging. The sun was just peeking through the buildings. I had high hopes for today. A long time ago, my therapist gave me a list of ten things to do when life got too overwhelming. I'd reached number seven by the time I found a seat on the train. It was going to be okay, I repeated internally. I tucked my legs under the bench and pretended to read on my phone while avoiding all polite good morning nods and blatant stares. Most of the commuters kept to themselves, for which I was thankful. I closed my eyes and listened to the sounds around me. The city waking up was musical. The repetition of the clicking of the train on the rail joints was the percussion. Outside, the crescendo of the traffic punctuated by horns and honks invigorated me as we chugged by. The high and low voices in the train created a rumbling that made me smile. It was the melody of the commuter morning.

Since my route was different, the sounds were new and washed over me like a concert I was hearing for the first time. The announcer's reveille snapped me out of my trance. I stood up and grabbed the bar until the train swayed to a stop and the doors opened. I waited for the mad dash of people to push past me before I exited the car. I walked down the platform and dove into the throngs of people on the sidewalk scurrying to work. There was plenty of time to cover the three blocks to my destination, so I scouted the area and found a coffee shop across the street, a bakery down the block, two sandwich places, and a pizza joint. I still had a block to go. I already knew I would have to step up my workout routine just to keep the calories off. Deep-dish cheese pizza and chocolate chip cookies were my downfall. Thankfully, there weren't any doughnut shops nearby.

Thirty minutes early, I pushed through the doors and checked in. One of the security guards escorted me up to Banks & Tyler. He tipped his hat at me after he deposited me at their door. I wasn't sure if I should be flattered or insulted. Was the escort normal? I opened the glass door to an empty reception area. Nobody was at the front desk, so I found a chair and a week-old magazine and waited.

"You must be Lily Croft. Hi, I'm Amanda." A woman a few years younger than me slipped into the receptionist area quickly, quietly put her purse in her drawer, and booted up her computer. "I will be with you as soon as I send out a quick email."

I nodded when she looked at me for confirmation.

She was attractive with short black hair, dark eyes, and a

curvy body. I wished I had some of her curves. Being a size six was nice, but at five foot eight, that meant my curves were almost nonexistent. Any weight I gained went straight to my thighs and not where I wanted it to go. I was destined to look like a string bean the rest of my life. Amanda's lipstick was bright red and I wondered how she kept it from sticking to her teeth. I was constantly playing with my lips, especially when concentrating on a problem. If I wore lipstick, it would be smeared all over my face by the end of the day.

"Come on. I'll show you to your office and around the place so you know where to find everything."

I nodded at her and looked down at the floor when I followed her. It was hard to miss her shapely calves and thin ankles. Her legs were attractive and she wasn't afraid to show them off. Her tight skirt sat about two inches above her knee. Still fashionable and professional, but it flirted dangerously with impropriety. We headed to the other side of the office, stopping briefly here and there to introduce me to the people who were already working at their desks. I started my anxiety list over. I knew that I would remember everybody's name; I just didn't want to meet them. After eight introductions, suffering through a tour of a small kitchen with two coffee counters, and Amanda's fine Vanna White arm swooping reveal of three vending machines tucked in the corner of the kitchen, we finally reached my office. "Mr. Hoyt gets in about eight thirty, so I'll just let you read about our company. Our home page is up on the computer." She jotted down my password to get into my email and smiled at me on her way out the door.

"Thanks for your hospitality, Amanda." My voice was soft, so she cocked her ear toward me to hear better. When she realized I wasn't going to say anything else, she nodded and left. I exhaled deeply. That wasn't so bad. I cleared my throat a few times in case anybody else decided to make a guest appearance. I wanted my voice to be firm and audible. I looked at the sparsely decorated office and decided it would do. Nothing distracting. The view out of the windows wasn't going to be a problem either. They were blocked by other buildings. Unfortunately, that just meant the people in those buildings could see in.

I casually scrolled through the website even though I already knew everything about the company. After I was done sulking when my boss gave me this assignment, I studied the company. Its 2009 inception was slow and steady, but recently the company had boomed and they were experiencing growing pains. Too much, too fast. My job as an actuary was to solve their business problems and evaluate risks to the company. My specialty was corporate finance, but I was good at risk management. Math was a sure thing. It never lied or cared. It just told the truth, regardless of emotions. With my head down, my brain on overdrive, and zero breaks, I received my mathematics degree from Princeton in three and a half years. As long as I kept my mind working, I didn't think about my life before college. I had the same passion as before, only with a different outlet. A safer one.

An older man let himself into my office. "Good morning, Ms. Croft. I'm Darren Hoyt. I'm so glad you are here."

I smiled because he looked exactly how I pictured he would. I stood and shook his hand. "Thank you. I'm excited to get started." I was. I wanted to be done with this project so I could get back to my own job in my own house on my own time.

"Did Amanda give you the tour? Do you have any questions for me?"

"She did a great job. Just show me where I can collect the data and get started," I said. He gave me a list of files that were password protected on the server and gave me full access. "I'm just down the hall near the kitchen. Can I take you to lunch today?" he asked.

I knew he was only being kind. "It's okay. I'm sure since it's my first day I'll dive into all this and forget about eating. I like to stay focused, but thank you for the invitation." I knew it was rude to say no, but I at least had manners about it. He shrugged his shoulders and awkwardly left my office. My phone rang thirty seconds later.

"Lily Croft." I wasn't going to say Banks & Tyler because even though our companies shared board members, I didn't work there.

"It's Darren Hoyt. I didn't mention that if you need anything, please just give Amanda a call. She's very helpful and knows where hard copies of things are."

"Thank you, Mr. Hoyt." I hung up and submerged myself in the information. At ten I stopped to buy a bottle of water from the vending machine. I kept my head down to avoid interaction. When I returned to my office, I shut the door, closed the world out, and surrounded myself with numbers.

❖

I felt the music in my chest at the exact moment I heard it. It was just after six and I had finished my first day on a high. Nobody bothered me. Amanda knocked on my door at five to let me know it was quitting time and gave me all my credentials to allow me access into the building and the office whenever I wanted. I stayed another hour but decided I didn't want to walk the neighborhood after dark. I turned off my light and headed out. The sandwich shop at the corner had meatball subs on special and I grabbed one. That would be my dinner. I was going to take it home and share it with Clio, but when I heard the music, I decided to stay and eat it outside the shop at a rickety bistro table with a matching wrought iron chair. For the first time in years, I didn't tense up or want to run away. It was a captivating composition that I remembered learning when I was nine and had played with the Pittsburgh Symphony Orchestra. I listened. The pianist interpreted "Clair de Lune" beautifully, building the momentum throughout the first section. My heart raced as I willed them to nail it. When they caught up and corrected the hesitation, I fist pumped. It was the first time I was excited about music in over a decade. My palms were sweaty and my sandwich all but forgotten as I smiled up at the unknown musician who included me in their journey. I waited a few minutes, but no other sounds wafted from the open second-story window. I checked the time. Six thirty. I needed to get home to Clio. I saved him a meatball in a to-go bag and threw the rest of my trash away.

The train ride was not as frenzied as it had been that morning. The clacking and shifting of the train was more subdued, so I stopped counting clicks and thought about my day. The people in the office were nice enough and left me alone. The data was well managed, so pulling together the information I needed was going to be easy, just time consuming. And I couldn't forget the music on my way to the station. When was the last time I wanted to listen and count to a piece? Whoever was playing was very talented. For a flash of a moment, I wanted to play again. I wanted to move my fingers across the keys and bring out the passion that was from my different life, but the feeling left as quickly as it came.

CHAPTER TWO

There's cake if you want some." Amanda poked her head into my office without knocking.

I was annoyed at her lack of respect for my privacy. I needed quiet. I wasn't interested in balloons, or a piece of fancy cake, or in gathering around to sing "Happy Birthday" along with people I barely knew. I just wanted to do my job quietly, privately, and get out of there each day until the project was finished.

She backed away slowly. "I'm sorry. I should've knocked."

"No, Amanda, wait. I'm sorry. It's just hard to stay focused sometimes when there are a lot of distractions. Thank you for letting me know. I appreciate it."

Her return smile didn't reach her eyes. I was a jerk. "Okay. Well, just thought you might want to know." She closed the door with a little bit more force than necessary.

I sighed and looked at my watch. It was almost two. I'd missed lunch. I needed to stretch my legs and get something to eat. My energy was waning, and my irritability was off the chart. I probably could've used the sugar rush in the form of cake, but for me to go into the break room now would just be awkward. I grabbed my purse, left my suit jacket, and headed out. A week had passed and I hadn't heard any music from the second floor. To say I was intrigued by the place was an understatement. I walked by the building slowly, hoping to hear something. There were no identifying marks on the outside of it other than the number carved into the stone archway, so I wasn't sure if it was residential, or commercial, or both.

"Excuse me."

I turned to find an older woman trying to get around me, carrying far too many bags in her hands.

I jumped out of the way and offered to get the door for her, hoping to catch a glimpse of the place inside in the process. I trotted up the stairs and pulled the large brass handle toward me.

"Thank you so much," she said as she walked in. As luck would have it, she dropped several bags that I automatically swooped down and picked up.

"I'll carry these for you," I said. I gave her a sweet, trustworthy smile and followed her down the hall to a large, wooden antique desk directly in the middle of the foyer. Faded brown leather couches and threadbare wingback upholstered chairs flanked the desk. It was furniture that probably looked great in a library forty years ago, but age and wear had faded its luster a long time ago. "What is this place?" The marble floors and stairs were polished to a high shine, and I couldn't help but reach out to touch the dark cherrywood railing that twirled up the stairs. This place was gorgeous even if the furnishings were dull.

"This is the Leading Note Music Center. We introduce children to music who otherwise wouldn't have the opportunity. With so many cutbacks in music and arts in the public school system, most children will never know if they have an aptitude for playing instruments or understanding music." The lady took her bags from me and placed them on the desk.

"How do they even get here? Is it open to the public?" I

was so intrigued by this idea. It was the exact opposite of how I grew up, where instruments were handed to me first thing in the morning to play, and practice was required every night before bed.

"It certainly is. Would you like a tour?" She was sincere and so nice that I nodded even though I knew I should leave. Panic hadn't set in yet, but my hands were starting to sweat and I knew I was only a few minutes away from bolting. "Great. Down here we have a few general music rooms on the left." She opened up one room that housed a studio piano and several other instruments including trumpets, clarinets, and flutes. They were more than gently used, but she was proud of them, so I kept my thoughts to myself. "And on the right we have three music therapy rooms."

The rooms were all decorated differently. One room was painted in bold primary colors and had toys and bean bags scattered across the room. The other two were more subdued with pastel colors and furniture that was symmetrically placed. I instantly relaxed.

"Do you do a lot with music therapy?" It was always a subject I was interested in, but never pursued.

"We work mainly with Lurie Children's Hospital, but we have several young clients who obtain therapy here privately. Musical therapy has shown to be so helpful in healing and communicating with children who cannot speak or have difficulty speaking."

"Are you a therapist here or an instructor?" I asked when she guided me to the second floor.

"I'm Agnes Barnes, a therapist here, but if time allows, I do instruct. I teach some of the local kids." She turned when she introduced herself to me and I stumbled over my own name.

"Hi, Agnes. I'm Lily Croft." Croft was an old family

name, but not the one I was born with. After my meltdown, one of my therapists recommended I take a giant step away from music to get out of the limelight. I went so far as to change my name. Jillian Crest was a child prodigy, but Lily Croft preferred the simplicity of numbers. "I work over at B and T just down the street. I heard somebody playing a sonata here the other evening and had to stop and listen to it."

"The second floor has our concert hall. Every month, the children put on a concert for the public. Well, it's more of a talent show to raise money for the program. You should come. It's next Friday night. The music you heard was probably Hope. She stays late some nights and gives private lessons." Agnes opened the door to a room that had five rows of red, cushioned chairs that faced a beautiful baby grand piano. I rubbed my palms together to stop from shaking and started the list in my head. "Are you okay? You turned very pale."

"I just haven't eaten yet today. I should probably go and grab some lunch." I turned on my heel and headed down the stairs. Drops of sweat gathered on my back just above the waistline of my suit skirt. I needed to get out of the building.

Agnes followed me down the stairs. "Thank you for your help. Here, take one of the flyers in case you are interested. You are more than welcome to visit anytime."

I all but snatched the flyer out of her hand and thanked her as I pushed through the door. I stumbled down the block and quickly walked across the street to get away. I crossed against the light and several drivers honked out their frustrations as I dodged their cars. I didn't even look back at Agnes, afraid that she would see the crazy in me. I slipped into the pizza shop and dropped into an empty booth. How could something so beautiful still make me lose control? I was going to have to call Dr. Monroe. We had focused so hard on socialization and letting go of the angst associated with performing music that we forgot to focus on the instruments themselves. I always told her I was fine being around them, but after seeing a Steinway Model S baby grand tucked in the corner of their concert hall, I felt like I was back onstage and all of the breathing exercises she taught me went out the window.

"Dr. Monroe? Hi, it's Lily Croft. Do you have time for a session tonight?" I knew I was overreacting, but I was clawing for stability and I knew she would help me find solid ground. Again.

"Let me check my schedule." She paused for a few seconds. I squeezed my eyes shut and prayed she did. "Yes. Can you be here at six?"

I agreed and hung up, feeling relieved. I fanned out my blouse to offer some relief to my perspiring body. A waitress stopped by and I looked at her several seconds before I realized I was in the pizza place. I quickly ordered water, a salad, and breadsticks. Today was a carb day. I deserved it.

❖

"Leaving with the rest of us, huh?" Amanda held the elevator as I struggled to get there from the office door. Both of my bags knocked against my thighs as I desperately tried to not look awkward to her and the three other people waiting for me.

I had to rethink bringing everything to work with me. "Thanks. Yes, I have to be somewhere at six." I don't know why I felt the need to tell her. I wanted to fill the void and avoid judgmental eye contact from the people who were anxious to leave the building but had to wait for me.

"I'm glad to see you're leaving at a decent time. Big plans tonight?" She was only being friendly. I told myself to answer her like a normal person would.

"I wish. Just meeting an old friend. For dinner," I quickly added in case she thought I was bar hopping. I couldn't remember the last time I had a drop of alcohol. Maybe it was my college graduation. No, it was the one time I tried online dating. That whole event was a disaster. It was amazing at how inexperienced I was at everything normal in life. Put me in front of a computer and I was a whiz, but in front of people, I was a hot mess.

"That sounds like fun. I hope you have a great time," she said.

I was going to have to be nicer to her. She waved good-bye to me and headed to the garage. I checked my watch and headed in the opposite direction. I had twelve minutes to catch the train. It would take me an additional thirty minutes to get to Dr. Monroe's office, and I would still have time to spare. I hit the corner and stopped. The music. I heard it even over the beginning of rush hour honks and traffic congestion. It was beautiful. And frightening. I slowed my pace and listened. It was the same pianist as before. Hope. I heard the exact slight hesitation on the same key. Maybe that was her way of interpreting the note. I was a sonata snob. I used to strive for perfection. I played every song I knew with every possible pause, and found perfection with everything I played. That was my goal. That was why people paid a lot of money to see me perform. I'd forgotten what it was like to be imperfect.

I wondered if the woman sat at the piano because she loved the music or because she wanted to conquer it. There was a difference. I closed my eyes and leaned up against the building. I pictured her fingers fluttering over the keys and wondered if she played from memory or read the music. She was good, really good. I smiled when she was done. She was pleased with it because she quickly played a ditty that made me smile harder. I looked down at my watch. Crap. I'd missed the train. With regret, I headed down the block to catch the next one. As much as I enjoyed listening, I still had to figure out a way to be around a piano without losing my cool like I had earlier today.

CHAPTER THREE

You never heard me play." I was flat on my back on the couch with Clio resting heavily on my chest. I absently rubbed his torn ear and thought about my session with Dr. Monroe. It felt good coming clean with her, admitting what happened today. "I used to be good. It was a lifetime ago. Doc thinks I should hang out near a piano or maybe even go to a concert or two." I reached over and slowly, so I wouldn't disturb Clio, plucked the flyer Agnes gave me off the coffee table and read it out loud. "Join us in celebrating music as it was meant to be heard and appreciated." I'd showed it to Dr. Monroe, and she thought it might be a step in the right direction if I attended. I didn't have to stay if I felt stifled. "It sounds like it might be an okay event."

I liked how the organization was all about choice, not about force. Agnes said the children were there of their own accord and were excited to learn and perform in front of others. It wasn't the same as my story. Dr. Monroe encouraged me to go somewhere and hang around a piano. She wanted me to touch it but not play it. Just face my fears. I knew my fear was irrational, but that didn't stop my body from sweating profusely from every pore whenever I thought about sitting down and playing again.

During our session, she convinced me to download a keyboard app on my phone. We downloaded it together, but she left it up to me to open it. I looked at the square on my screen, but swiped past it. I'd get to it eventually. The power it already had over me was insane. I was angry at my own weakness. I tossed the flyer back on the table and promised myself I would at least show up. I owed it to myself. I grabbed Clio and padded off to the bedroom. I wanted to get in early tomorrow because crunching numbers helped me forget about everything else. I also wanted to leave at five, not because I was done working for the day, but because maybe I would hear the music again.

❖

"You're making great progress, Lily." Mr. Hoyt popped into my office with a big smile. He, too, didn't knock, and the look I shot him told him he should have. "I'm sorry. I didn't mean to interrupt you."

I waved him in because he was technically my boss. I just wished he would have scheduled a time to meet and review rather than just barge in. "It's fine. Come on in. I take it you saw the report I emailed you?" I was surprised because I'd just sent it ten minutes ago, and it required a lot more time to review. I'd either underestimated him or he'd overestimated me.

"I sent it to the team for review. I'm just here to delegate. And play golf on nice days." He winked at me.

I still couldn't read him, but he did have a certain charm that warmed me. I decided he was smarter than he led people to believe. He was the Senior Actuary, Annuities Director. One didn't achieve that status by joking around and playing sports on workdays. He had to have put in some serious time and effort. I just hadn't seen it. I'd only been working three weeks and always beat him in and left after he did. I was almost halfway through the project and on target to finish two weeks early. My real boss, Gene, told me to double-check everything and take the full eight weeks. I'm sure that had more to do with billable hours and less with my own health and sanity.

"If you have any questions, I'll be more than happy to answer them." I didn't know how to be social with him. Numbers were safe. Small talk wasn't.

"You should take more breaks, walk around, get to know the people here. This is a great company to work for. And it looks like we'll be here a while." He was proud, and rightfully so. Their growing pains were the good kind to have.

I had a few financial ideas for them besides the obvious hiring more employees. Teaching employees how to forecast catastrophic events and how to distribute the money in advance for them was like herding cats. It was all projections based on what-ifs, and people got nervous around money. A lot of money. But there was repetition in numbers and history, and that's what made my job easy. I was there to review the data and design a training program that allowed the adjusters to do their job without bankrupting the company. People trusted the assuredness in my reports.

"Oh, I'm sure the employees are great. I just wanted to get started right away. There's so much information to process that it's hard to get away from it once you dig in. You know what that's like. I suppose I could get up and take more breaks." I kept talking until I saw his shoulders relax. My last suggestion seemed to appease him.

"Pick a day next week. We'll do lunch. That gives you plenty of time." He winked at me and left my office. It was hard not to like him. It was as if he knew my struggles. Then again, it wasn't as if our field was full of social people.

"Okay. I'll check my calendar and get back to you," I said even though he was already gone. I figured he heard me down the hall since he left my door wide open. I really hadn't spoken to a lot of people here. Amanda, Mr. Hoyt, Josh the intern who was bound and determined to wear me down and be my friend, and Hannah the mail distributor who never had mail for me but was always nice and said hello when she wheeled her cart past my office. I needed to try harder. At least the people here seemed friendlier than the people I saw every Friday at my permanent job. Those people resented that I worked from home and only had to make an appearance one day a week. The employees here didn't know me well enough yet.

I sat back in my chair and closed my eyes for a minute. I had been hunched over the computer for hours, and my shoulders and neck were sore. My feet hated the heels I'd picked out that morning. The shoes gave me height but also pinched my toes. I'd forgotten how hellish they were to wear until I got halfway to the train.

I kicked the shoes off, curled my feet underneath me, and decided to check my email on my phone. I refused to use the computer at work for anything other than the project I was assigned. I didn't want to leave a digital trail. As I was just about to hit the mail app, my emotions hijacked my brain and hit the piano app instead. I clutched my phone as I watched it spool open. There in front of me were black and white keys. I took a deep breath and emotionally pushed myself to touch a key. Nothing happened. I was both relieved and confused. I hit it again. Still nothing. My glorious comeback to piano-land was a dud.

I groaned when I noticed I had my phone on silent. I turned the volume on, took another deep breath, and hit the D key. The quality of the sound was horrific, but I didn't panic right away. No, the freak-out happened about ten notes later when I realized I had played a scale. I closed out of the app and quickly stood. I told myself to relax. I was in charge of this. Nobody else. I stared down at my phone and saw only my reflection in the black screen. Perfect time for a break. I got up, slipped my angry shoes back on, left my phone behind, and headed for the kitchen. I had a raspberry yogurt with my name on it in the communal refrigerator. I walked into the break room and froze when six people turned to stare at me.

"Hi, Lily." Josh's smile was friendly as he ushered me into the room.

I wanted to ninja slink out, but instead I pasted on a smile and continued my trek to grab my snack. "Hi, Josh. How are you?"

"Good. Glad to see you out and about. Got plans tonight?" Dear God, I hoped he wasn't asking me out. "We're going to shoot pool down at Bleachers tonight. You in?"

"I'm not good at pool, and as inviting as it sounds, I really can't. I have another project at home that I need to finish." He looked disappointed but not dejected. I was actually great at pool. Even though there was a tiny part of me that wanted to go, I wasn't dressed for anything but work.

"Well, we might be in a tournament on Friday night as well, so keep that night open if you want."

I smiled and nodded on my way out of the kitchen. I planned on attending the concert at the Leading Note and needed the rest of the week to work up the courage to actually go.

CHAPTER FOUR

You made it. It's good to see you again." Agnes's genuine smile made me relax a little bit. My body was rigid and my hands were sweating, but I was there and making an effort. "There are a few seats in the back row."

I swore she read my mind. The seat closest to the door was taken, so I took the spot two seats down, leaving the seat between me and an older gentleman vacant. We exchanged smiles and I looked down at my phone to avoid a possible conversation. I had ten minutes to kill and no idea how to do it.

I wasn't a people watcher and I didn't want to talk to anyone, so I pulled up CNN on my phone and looked at the financial section. I liked playing the stock market. Just for fun, I'd opened a trading account a year ago and had been hooked ever since. It wasn't a passion, more of a hobby. My money from when I played was heavily invested in retirement options. I wasn't going to touch it for decades. This was just spending money. Fun money for vacations I never took and expensive clothes I never bought.

"If everyone would please take a seat, we'll get started. Thank you for coming tonight. It's nice to see familiar faces and some new ones. My name is Hope D'Marco. This is one of our favorite events here at the Leading Note. Tonight's theme is Evening and we are going to start the concert off with Tyson Watts, who is going to play the 'Sleeping Beauty Waltz.'"

Hope D'Marco. I couldn't take my eyes off her. Her gaze held mine for a fraction of a second when her eyes scanned the crowd during her introduction. I looked around to see if anybody else felt the spark in the room or heard the booming noise that echoed in my ears. My heart was twirling in my chest, free-falling into an unknown abyss. I was surrounded by a crowd of smiling people—parents, grandparents, and other children—but none of them mattered. Hope D'Marco, with her long chestnut hair and dark brown eyes, commanded my attention. It was several notes into the composition before I even realized Tyson, a boy about twelve years old, was playing. He flubbed up several times but never gave up, and was smiling when he was done. The room erupted with applause. He playfully bowed and joined his family in the front row. Hope stood center stage again and introduced the next student, an eight-year-old violinist who tackled "Minuet in G Major" and also did a decent job. I watched Hope sit behind the student and bob her head encouragingly at the notes. The violinist, too, was applauded by the audience when they bowed.

So, this was what it was supposed to be like—positive reinforcement, smiles, mistakes, and laughter. When Hope sat at the piano to accompany a young cellist, I stood up. She hesitated when we made eye contact again. I forced myself to sit and stay. I took a deep breath and clutched the cushioned seat to keep myself calm. The weight in my hands gave me comfort. The metal frame against my fingertips was a cool point of contact against my warm body. Hope nodded at Liam and they began "Melody in A Flat Major" by Louise Farrenc. I was mesmerized. Hope accompanied him in perfect rhythm. I wasn't sure when I started crying, but I gratefully accepted the tissue from the old man's outstretched hand. I dabbed my eyes, but more tears poured out. When the composition ended and the entire audience jumped to their feet, I raced out of the room and ran down the stairs as quickly as I could. I wasn't prepared to be that emotional. I walked two blocks before the tears stopped and I felt normal again. I took another deep breath, shook my arms down at my sides to release the tension in my body. I smiled because I survived it. It wasn't as bad as I thought. I walked another block before I realized I was walking in the opposite direction from the train station.

I looked around to get my bearings and saw Bleachers, the bar Josh mentioned, and headed there to celebrate. I hoped he was still there. It was only seven thirty. I opened the door and was greeted by loud voices and the smell of fried foods. It took a few seconds for my eyes to adjust to the dimness.

"Lily. Hey, Lily. Over here." I heard to my left. Josh waved me over. I recognized three other people from work and smiled. "You made it. Want a beer?" Josh was already pouring one for me even though I wanted a water.

"Sure. Thanks." I sat on the empty seat he pulled out from a nearby high-top.

"You want to play? We are just warming up." He thrust a pool stick into my hand and pointed at the felt. "Show us what you got."

I shrugged and put my beer down on the high tabletop. Thankfully, my blouse was buttoned all the way up to my throat so when I bent over, I wasn't giving the room a show. My clothes were modest. I just wished I didn't look so square.

"Stripes or solids?" Either way, I was going to sink at least three balls.

"Stripes. Sean already dropped a solid in," he said.

I nodded and focused. When I sank the first one, they cheered. By the fourth one, they were all quiet, except Josh.

He was doing a celebratory dance with tiny yapping noises until the end of my run.

"You said you sucked at pool." Josh laughed and scooped up the money that teetered on the edge of the pool table. He tried handing me half, but I declined.

"Hustler. I call foul," Sean said. He toasted me anyway.

I giggled and decided I really needed to eat. The beer, probably my fourth alcoholic drink ever, went straight to my head. I waved over a waitress and ordered a cheeseburger, fries, and a large water that I gulped down when she returned with it.

"What do you do for the company, Sean?" I asked. My feeble attempt at conversation was at least safe. Sean was probably ten years older than the rest of us but acted a lot younger. Josh, Benton, and Allison, adjusters for B&T, were all close to my twenty-seven years. We talked a little about the business, and for the first time ever, I didn't feel awkward. Credit the beer. Plus, I mainly just listened to them and smiled. I was a part of something that, even just for a short time, wasn't uncomfortable.

When my food arrived, Sean and Josh reached over and ate some of my fries. They didn't ask, but I didn't care. It was so smooth and I wondered if this was what having friends was like. I'd been homeschooled because of my music career, so I didn't have any friends growing up. In college, I was friendly with my roommate my freshman year, but the rest of the time, I lived alone.

"So, tell us about yourself, Lily. You're so elusive at work." Josh wiggled his fingers at me in a ghostlike fashion accompanied by a *woo* noise.

The heat crept across my face. I covered my mouth while I swallowed a large bite. "Not much to tell. I work for Banks Corporation across town, I have a cat named Clio, and I read a lot." I shrugged my shoulders like I was no big deal because I really wasn't. Not anymore.

"Come on, are you married? Dating anyone?" Sean had a wedding ring and a ton of photos of his kids on his phone that we'd already seen.

I shook my head. "No. Taking a break from it all." I almost snorted at my boldfaced lie. I had no interest in men and had only one quasi-relationship in college with a teacher's aide. Carrie was clingy from day one. I needed space more than I needed a relationship. We lasted a couple of months. I was still a virgin.

"My boyfriend and I are taking a break. We are still technically together, but he needs a breather." Josh air-quoted the word "breather."

I didn't see that coming. Not that I had gaydar, but I never got that vibe from him. In the first week, I thought he was hitting on me. The relief that washed over me was liberating. He was not into me. Allison shared that she had a long-distance boyfriend who lived in Indianapolis. The guys teased her because they never met him, but she pulled out her phone and showed us all photos of them kissing and holding one another, and a thousand other selfies.

"You can't fake that." Josh threw up his hands. "Okay, fine, you have a boyfriend." Allison smiled dreamily at Josh, probably because she was thinking about Patrick.

"When will you see him again?" I asked.

"Not for two more weeks."

"So, that makes us responsible for entertaining you until then, right?" Sean asked wickedly and leaned up against her. She playfully nudged him away.

"Don't you have a wife and like seventeen kids to go home to?" Allison threw back at him.

Sean looked at his watch and jumped up. "You're right.

I'm out. Have a fun rest of your night. Nice to finally meet you, Lily."

I wasn't expecting that. It was nice. I waved at him and watched as he left. Just as I turned in my chair to rejoin the conversation in progress, my eye caught Hope and Agnes walking into Bleachers. I froze. I couldn't stop staring.

"You all right?" A smiling Josh leaned into my line of vision, breaking up my trance.

"What? Oh, yeah. I'm fine." The cheeseburger churned in my stomach. I reached for my second beer because I was out of water again. I gulped it to settle my nerves. What were they doing here? Logically eating after the concert, but why here? I turned back to face Josh and Allison and pasted on a smile.

"Well, with Sean gone, I guess we won't be able to participate in the tournament, but at least now we have a ringer. An ace in the hole," Josh said.

What had I started? Tonight was a fluke. I happened to be in the area and walked in on a whim. I couldn't imagine doing this twice a week or however often they met and played.

"I'm only at B and T for another month, so you'll probably have to get your hands on another player and not count on me."

"How far away do you live?" Allison asked.

"It takes me a good hour by train just to get here every day."

"That's about normal for us," Josh said. He and Allison both lived north of the city. Neither had cars and relied solely on public transportation.

I couldn't imagine that kind of commute for the rest of my life. I didn't have a car either, but I never went anywhere. The internet delivered everything I needed, as did the grocery store down at the corner. If it wasn't for having to make an appearance every Friday at Banks Corporation, I would consider myself a hermit.

"Hi, Lily. I'm glad you showed up tonight." Agnes touched my shoulder and I had no choice but to turn and face her. It was only her. Hope was seated at a high-top across the room.

"It was great. Thank you for the invitation. I'm sorry I didn't stay the entire concert." I nervously fiddled with my napkin in my lap and hoped she would just leave.

"It's all right. It was a great turnout, and it's always nice to see new people," she said.

"Hi, I'm Josh."

I rolled my eyes at my lack of manners.

"I work with Lily. So do Benton and Allison." He nodded at Allison and she smiled hello at Agnes before getting back into her texting conversation with her boyfriend.

"I'm Agnes. I work at the Leading Note Music Center just a few blocks down. We had a concert this evening. Now we're out for some much-needed adult time." She pointed over to Hope, who smiled at us.

"You and your friend should sit with us. Do either of you play pool?" Josh asked.

I wanted to punch Josh. I sat up straighter when Agnes waved Hope over to the table. How did I look? I wiped my lips with my napkin in case I had ketchup in the corners of my mouth. What if I had lettuce stuck in my teeth? There wasn't anything I could do about that now. Nothing seemed out of the ordinary. I watched as Hope weaved around the other bar tables to reach us. I tried not to stare when she approached us, but it was futile. Her looks commanded attention. Up close, she was more beautiful than I imagined. More than I could take. I looked down at my plate, suddenly very interested in a pickle slice, the only thing left besides a small dab of ketchup.

"Hi. I'm Hope."

"Lily and her friends invited us over. Lily was at the concert tonight," Agnes said.

"Thanks for inviting us over."

I was jealous of how comfortable she was with everyone. Her hair was down but tucked behind her ears, which showed off her creamy, flawless skin. Two tiny dimples flashed across her cheeks when she smiled at Josh and Allison. When our eyes met again, I had to look down at my plate. I was either going to have to eat this pickle or make it my pet. I was spending entirely too much time concentrating on it.

"Thanks for coming to the concert, Lily," she said to me.

I had to look at her. "I heard you practicing 'Clair de Lune' the other day. The measure before the key signature change needs considerable practice to make the transition smooth. It's a difficult section to master." Now why the fuck would I say that to her, to anyone? I couldn't stop. "You are so close. At one point, you nailed it, but I think with more practice you will get—" With great effort, I stopped myself. "What I meant to say was that the concert tonight was great and I enjoyed hearing the kids play." My voice trailed off.

"Yeah, I struggle with that piece. I just have a hard time pacing myself on that section. Was it that obvious?" She was so sincere, I felt like the world's biggest ass. I reached out to touch her forearm but pulled back before we actually connected.

"No, no. I'm sorry. I shouldn't have said anything. Just keep practicing and you'll master it. You're a very good pianist. You made me cry at the concert tonight. I used up every single tissue within a five-chair radius. I'm just sorry I left. I had to."

She nodded as if she understood me.

"What kind of concert?" Josh asked. He waved the waitress over for another pitcher of beer and poured the last of what we had left in two glasses for Hope and Agnes.

"A little classical concert that our students put on once a month."

"Oh, the classical music school. You moved in earlier this year, right?" Josh asked. Agnes nodded. "I like the music I've heard there. I used to play the clarinet in high school. Is it just for kids or is it for adults, too?"

"It's mostly for students around the area, middle school age and younger." Hope's voice was so smooth and gentle. "A lot of high schools still have their music programs, but most elementary and middle schools have ended their arts programs. Our organization helps kids match up with instruments and gives them the opportunity to learn something new and have fun doing it."

I heard pride and wondered how she got her position there. Was it in the family? She obviously knew how to play. I was curious at her background.

"How long have you been playing?" I asked. That was a safe question. I forced myself to make eye contact with her while I waited for her answer. I clutched my cloth napkin under the table. That helped settle my anxiety.

"Since I was about eleven. I was in dance before that, but I told my parents that I wanted to try music. My mom took me to the symphony and asked what three instruments I liked the most. I picked the piano, the flute, and the harp."

She smiled at me and I looked down at my plate. That fucking pickle! I grabbed my plate and handed it to a waitress walking by. She wasn't ours, but I needed to get the plate away from me. I had no excuse now so I had to maintain eye contact.

"Which is your favorite? I know the harp is pretty complex even though it looks simple." I knew firsthand how the harp, as beautiful as it sounded, was a bitch to play at a high standard.

She shifted in her chair to look directly at me. "I really

enjoy tackling all of them. When I give lessons, I'm still learning. There are so many different ways to interpret music and sometimes the students teach me things." Zing. I deserved that.

"So, now tell me about the Leading Note," I said.

It was an opportunity to study Hope the way I wanted. Gone was the braid that draped across her left shoulder during the concert. I liked the way her hair flowed in waves halfway down her back. It was a few inches longer than my own and several shades darker. The short-sleeved red sweater she wore accentuated her slight tan. I wondered if she'd just vacationed somewhere tropical. Did she travel with someone? A boyfriend? A girlfriend? Her jeans were fashionably tight and the simple black flats on her feet completed her girl-next-door look. She wore her watch with the face resting on the underside of her slender wrist. I wondered if she did that on purpose, or if it had a way of slipping throughout the day and she simply gave up.

Hope D'Marco brought elegance to this bar. I listened as she explained how she studied music in college but just wasn't good enough to make it her career. Instead, she got in with a company that designed and sold cell phone apps. It was a cutthroat business, but it gave her enough money to start the Leading Note four years ago. In my head, that put her at about thirty years old.

"How are you funded? If that's not too personal." Oh, look, my manners made an appearance. The question involved money and math, so it was a comfortable topic for me. I just needed to be aware of my delivery. I think I blurted out the question, but the music was getting louder and it was harder to hear. Also, the beer wasn't helping with my much-needed filter, but it was soothing my nerves. I scooted my stool closer to her.

"Foundations, grants, donations. I spend all of my non-

LISTEN
teaching time with my hand out for money." She shrugged like it wasn't a big deal, but behind that easygoing facade was a hardworking woman.

Running an organization was not for the laid back. I was enthralled with her. Not only was she beautiful, physically and musically, but she was so comfortable with herself, even around other people.

"We also get donations, and health insurance companies pay us for the work we do with patients."

I nodded at her. I wanted to know everything. Everything about the organization, about Hope. Hell, even Agnes intrigued me. After Josh hijacked the conversation, I sneaked quick looks at her and had the decency to blush when she caught me. When Agnes made eye contact with Hope and pointed at her watch, I almost groaned. Don't go. Tonight is such a big night for me, I thought. They said good-bye and Hope thanked us for inviting them over. I watched them walk out and sighed heavily at their departure. I wasn't close to being done with questions. When was the last time I wanted to spend time with another person?

"Lily." I felt a warm hand on my forearm that startled me. I turned to find Hope completely in my personal space, and I was surprisingly okay with it.

"Hi, you're back." I could tell my smile was cheesy and entirely too large for a casual hey.

"I wanted to give you my business card. Please stop by anytime and we can talk more about the organization, or just talk."

I held the card in my hand and stared at it for however long. When I looked up, she was still standing beside me, waiting for a reply.

"Thank you, I will." Her smile was warm and softer than before. I felt like it was reserved just for me.

• 43 •

CHAPTER FIVE

If you're going to stand there and judge me, you might as well come up and do it in person."

I looked up, completely busted. How did Hope know I was down here? She was smiling down at me from the open window, so I knew she was kidding, but I still felt guilty. I was judging her. Silently, but also encouragingly.

"I really should go home and feed Clio." That was the first thing that popped out of my mouth. I had to look down because my neck was hurting from looking directly up at Hope, and the sun was reflecting off the windows and blinding me.

"Is Clio your dog?" she asked playfully. Was she flirting?

"He's my cat. He's on a pretty strict schedule."

"Come on up for a quick minute and say hi."

"I really can't. I'm sorry." I still wasn't ready to be in a room with a piano, let alone, in a room with a beautiful woman playing it.

"Can you do dinner? Clio would understand, I'm sure."

I gulped. Could I be alone with Hope and make small dinner conversation? Baby steps. At least a piano wasn't involved. And I hadn't eaten since the bagel I wolfed down about ten that morning.

"I think if we do something quick, that will work." Could

I be a bigger ass right now? A beautiful woman I admired was asking me to dinner. "I mean, sure. Do you know of a good place close by?" That sounded better. I looked down at my trousers and short-sleeved blouse. I'd recently found myself dressing a tad nicer for the just-in-case moments. This was one of them. Not that I would have chosen this outfit for a first date, but it was cute. Wait. Was this a date?

"I know a place. Give me a minute to lock up."

She closed the window and disappeared. Holy shit. Talk about impromptu. At least I'd slept the night before and still looked decent. The surge of energy bubbled over and I started pacing in front of the door. Remember the steps, I told myself. I counted to ten, I took five deep breaths and thought about everything else except Hope D'Marco. The project I was working on would be done in two weeks. I needed to remember to call the vet and refill Clio's prescription. He also needed more food. There was something else about food. Did I need to bring food for the company barbecue on Friday? I thought of everything I could to keep my mind off her, but when she stood in front of me, everything else faded away. The traffic, all the noise, the people rushing by us were gone. Hope's smiling face was the only thing I saw.

"Are you ready?" she asked. I nodded and she pointed behind us. "There's a cute little diner that's just a few blocks east of here. So, you work at B and T, right?"

"I work for Banks Corporation, which has some ownership of B and T. They sent me over to review their business and advise B and T on a few things. I'll be out of here in a few weeks or so. Banks Corp is on the other side of town." I tried to keep it light because describing my job almost always ensured a stifled yawn from the listener. Very few people knew or cared what an actuary did.

"It's too bad that you won't be around. I was hoping for

more musical advice." I was glad Hope didn't press me on how I knew so much about the piano. "Maybe you can swing by anyway. We like visitors. They help get the word out about this place. We moved in six months ago. It's not the greatest location for the kind of traffic we want, but our lease was up at the old place and this was what we could find on such short notice."

"Where were you before?" It wasn't as if I'd been a lot of places, but I'd learned the city by studying and memorizing maps. It was comforting to have a general knowledge of my surroundings.

"Closer to Edgewater. It's so hard to get a quality, affordable place where we want, so we buy bus and train passes for some of our less fortunate students. This is a difficult location because there aren't too many neighborhood kids that know about us yet and can just hang out. Our old place was perfect, but they raised the rent so much last minute that we just couldn't afford it."

I could tell that she was really upset by the move, and I understood. Kids needed stability and something they could always count on. The center moving probably crushed their spirits and took away their hands-on musical outlet. Music appreciation started at such a young age, and a lot of times, children weren't given the opportunity to listen and learn it.

"I'm surprised you're here, this close to businesses. Then again, people live everywhere in Chicago," I said. My condo was in a very nice part of the city. I was fortunate, but it came with a price. My childhood had been nonexistent, but it afforded me luxuries now.

"It's not a bad place, just not easily accessible to kids. I wish we were closer to schools." She held the door open for me once we reached Twenty Four, a diner wedged between two taller buildings.

I blushed at her consideration. "Thank you," I stammered. I felt the softness of her body as she brushed past me to talk to the hostess. I grabbed the handle of my purse tighter as the need to be closer to her overwhelmed me. I never wanted to be close to people. Hope D'Marco was different. She made me feel happy, a feeling I hadn't had in years. Even when I was alone with Clio, it wasn't happiness I felt. It was peace. Clio relaxed my world. Hope gave it excitement. I needed those two to meet.

"Let's go." Hope looked back at me and nodded toward the hostess, who was walking to the back of the diner. Hope waited for me to pick a side of the booth and sat across from me. This felt like a date. I clutched my purse tighter. "So, everything here is good, if you are into comfort food."

I grabbed the menu and looked at the specials. "I'm certain I could eat one of everything." My stomach gurgled when I saw meatloaf on the menu. In my mind, I settled for the salad. Once I realized Hope was going to order the fried chicken meal, I threw in the towel and ordered the special: meatloaf, mashed potatoes, gravy, and green beans. I sipped on my unsweetened ice tea. I was excited for so many different flavors.

"This place is great. I've only eaten here a few times, but the food is wonderful and the atmosphere is so laid back," she said.

She looked adorable today. I loved her hair down. She was wearing jeans and a really cute blouse. I wasn't a jeans person, but Hope had such a nice body that she made jeans look classy. She accessorized nicely with a thin silver necklace, two bracelets, and the watch that rested on the inside of her wrist. Upon closer inspection, that was just how she wore it. It made me smile. The face was bold and slightly bigger than I expected someone with her petite frame to wear.

"You're wondering about my watch."

I looked back to her and held her gaze. "The first time I saw you, I wondered if it slipped down or if that was just the way you wore it."

She fingered the weathered band and ran her fingertip over the crystal face. I could tell her mind was elsewhere, but just for a flash. She turned to me and smiled. "It was my grandfather's. I know it's kind of big and clunky for me, but I feel close to him when I wear it."

Even though I didn't speak with my parents, I checked in with my grandparents from time to time. They were the only ones who tried to intervene when they sensed I was slipping. "Did he pass away?"

The corners of her mouth tilted up at a memory and fell at the reality of the truth. "He died in a car crash. He swerved to avoid hitting a truck that had stalled around a curve in the road and ended up hitting a telephone pole. It was dark, and raining, and cold. I remember it was so cold that night."

"You were there?"

She nodded. "I was buckled up in the back seat. We were singing a song. He was always singing. It was great." She was sad, but the whisper of a smile ghosted her lips.

"How old were you?"

"I was twelve and walked away without a scratch. My grandfather stayed alive until the police showed up. I believe that he hung around until he knew I was safe. He tried to keep up a brave front, but I knew he was in a lot of pain." She absentmindedly drew a design with the tip of her spoon on the pattern of the vinyl tablecloth. She was lost in her thoughts, so I waited. I knew what that was like. It gave me a chance to study her. Her skin was flawless except for a tiny scar just at her temple. I admired her forearms and hands. They were strong and lean. When she looked up at me, I leaned back at the intensity I saw in her eyes. I wasn't used to one-on-one attention, especially from a beautiful woman.

"Do you come from a large family?" I often wondered what that was like. I only knew the large families from television or movies. Once my parents realized I could play music, they stopped trying to have more children and focused their attention solely on me, for all of the wrong reasons.

"I'm the baby. I have three older brothers," she said. I didn't know why I laughed, but she joined in. "Yeah, it's ridiculous. I had to blackmail them into letting me do things as a teenager. They were under strict orders to keep me in line, and every single one made sure I knew it." Her smile was warm so I knew it was all out of love.

"Do they all live here in the Chicago area?" I wondered what it was like to be under what I considered good scrutiny.

"I have one brother in New York, but the other two are close by. I see them on Sundays. That gives me a chance to hang out with my nieces and nephews, who thankfully take after their mothers." She grinned.

Our food arrived and the conversation shifted to it.

"I'm so glad I went with the meatloaf. This smells heavenly. Yours looks just as delicious." I pointed my fork at her plate. The fact that I was going to eat in front of her was amazing. Public eating wasn't a thing for me. First the cheeseburger at Bleachers, and now this.

"Tell me about Clio," she said.

The warm food relaxed me and I found myself far more open with her than I had been when I was drinking. I smiled when she mentioned his name.

"Clio is my true love. He's an alley cat that started hanging around me. One day I heard something in my window and was surprised to see him outside on my fire escape. I'm on the eighth floor. He was there for a reason." I didn't elaborate, and Hope didn't push. "Do you have any pets?"

"I wish. I just don't have the time. I love dogs, but the city isn't the greatest place for them, so I just love them from afar. I do like cats, but I'm slightly allergic to them," she said.

"So you can never come back to my place," I said, thinking of Clio. When the words I'd just spoken out loud sank into my thick skull, I blushed and stammered a correction. "I mean, you know, Clio is kind of fluffy, and I'm sure his dander would bother you. That's, ah, what I meant." I took a bite of meatloaf so I wouldn't have to look at her.

"Never? That's sad," she said.

My heart raced and playfully skipped around inside my chest. She made me feel like a schoolgirl with a crush. I had zero experience with flirting, so I wasn't sure if she was interested in me, or was just being nice. Either way, it made me feel special.

"Well, I mean, sure, if you wanted to, but I know how difficult allergies can be." I mentally told myself to clean the apartment from top to bottom and maintain it for the just-in-case moment Hope showed up. I realized I needed to change the subject or else I would obsess about cleaning, and the goal was to act normal. "You have nieces and nephews. That must be nice. I'm an only child, so I'll never have that."

"Do you want children?" She was so attentive that I felt myself tensing up when I noticed her body leaning forward, her eyes on mine, and all of the classic signs that told me she was interested in me, engrossed in hearing what I had to say. That made me nervous.

"I'm not really mother material," I said.

She scoffed. "Yes, you are. You are young, successful,

and you're intelligent." I squirmed in my seat at her praise. "Plus, you know music better than anybody else I know. You fixed my problems in two sentences. Two. You have a lot to offer. You would be a good mom." The gentleness in her voice told me she was serious. What did Hope know about me? She didn't know my mental problems, my breakdown, or my everyday struggles.

I was getting worked up over nothing. "What about you? You work with kids every day. Does that make you want to have them, or is that enough for now?" The fact that I could even talk to her right then was a major breakthrough. Nine times out of ten, I would have jumped up and left. Her face, her demeanor, calmed me. My nervousness was for something entirely different. I was being torn between running away from sheer anxiety and staying strictly out of curiosity. What was happening here? What was going to happen here? Did I just find a friend, or was there more going on? I had no experience in friendships and only a few months of dating experience. I hoped I wasn't reading her wrong.

"I'm sure once I find the perfect woman, we'll settle down and talk about kids. I'm all for having them, but if she isn't, I'm not going to be devastated."

My stomach lurched at her confession. So much was going on in that sentence that I stood up and excused myself for a minute. I headed toward the restrooms and paced the tiny hallway. Little beads of sweat popped up at my temple. I felt my pulse beat hard against my neck and covered my throat with my hand to try to relax. I was at the beginning stages of a panic attack. Hope was single and was looking. She was also a lesbian, which was something I dreamed of but never thought I would hear from her lips. I didn't know how to process the information, so I kept pacing.

"Are you okay?"

I felt soft hands on my upper arms and started to shrink away. She immediately released me when our eyes met.

"Um, yes. I was just headed back to the table." How long was I gone? The same people were sitting in booths around us, so I guessed not very long. "I'm sorry about that."

She nodded and walked behind me, careful not to touch me, but close enough that I could reach out to her if I needed to. "I just wanted to make sure you didn't bail and stick me with the bill." She winked at me. Hope was the first woman who made me feel both completely nervous and at ease at the same time.

"I can be a jerk, but I would never do that to you," I said.

She reached out and carefully touched my hand after we sat back down. It took all of my energy not to shrink away. Not because I didn't want her to touch me, but because I did. I wasn't used to contact unless it was Clio. I found that I wanted it desperately, and that scared me. I looked down at the rose-colored manicured nails that rested on the knuckles of my left hand. I felt the soft calluses on her fingertips and knew they came from a guitar or a cello, something she had recently picked up after a long absence or just started to play. Chill bumps raced up my arm, and I prayed that she didn't see them.

"You are not even close to being a jerk, okay? You're sweet and kind. Just a little nervous," she said.

"I...um. I'm just not used to people. I know that makes me sound weird." I had no other explanation.

She squeezed my hand. "Not weird. I get it. Not everybody is an extrovert. There are some days even I don't like people."

I frowned when she pulled her hand away from mine. I missed her warmth immediately. "That's why Clio is so good for me. We understand one another." My appetite was gone. I wanted to go home and curl up with him.

"Maybe you have room in your life for one more." She said it with such conviction that for a few moments I believed this could happen. That somehow, someway, this woman could be, wanted to be, a part of my life.

CHAPTER SIX

When Banks & Tyler had a company barbecue, they went all out. They opened up the large conference room, and every single employee brought something to eat. I brought potato salad from the deli near my house. At first I wasn't going to participate, but Josh kept asking until I committed. I had no idea why we were having a barbecue, but it put everybody in a good mood. I was slinking back to my office after fixing a plate but stopped when Amanda blocked my path.

"Did you make this potato salad? It's scrumptious."

"I wish I could take credit, but I don't cook. What's the occasion today?" I wasn't on the office email system, so I wasn't sure why or what we were celebrating. I figured if it was important, somebody would tell me. Several of the guys went up on the roof to grill burgers, hot dogs, and chicken. I didn't even know we had roof access. Apparently it was a nice setup. I would have to check it out sometime.

"It's the company anniversary. We do this every year. With the weather so nice, it's hard to keep everybody indoors. You should head up there and check it out. There's a bar, shuffleboard, life-size chess board, and an herb garden. It's really cool."

I nodded and skirted around her, anxious to get back to

my office. I shut the door and called my boss over at Banks Corporation. I told him I would be done by this time next week. I was even stretching out the time because I knew he was going to be disappointed at how fast I'd done the job. And, truthfully, I felt pangs of sadness because I was just starting to make eye contact and smile with some of the employees here. Banks & Tyler was an easier place to work. There was a level of comfort that didn't exist at Banks Corporation.

"Hoyt says he's pleased with your analysis," Gene said. Even though he couldn't see me, I nodded. I knew my work here was solid. "Why don't you take a few days off when you are done?"

"I don't mind the work," I said.

"If only all of my employees could be like you, Lily." He hung up and I leaned back in my chair. This project, however simple it was, had changed me. I'd done consulting projects before, but I felt another shift happening inside me. Slower this time, and definitely positive.

I was sure it was because of meeting Hope. Our dinner the other night was nice and gave me a sliver of confidence. Maybe there was something there. Hell, I was happy to just develop a friendship, but I was also hopeful. When was the last time I kissed a woman? I tried online dating one night years ago. At the end of the date, the girl practically threw herself at me. The kiss was sloppy and almost made me gag. The time before that was college. It wasn't that I didn't want a relationship, because I desperately did, I just never thought I could survive the courtship. Hope had a way of calming my nerves while keeping me teetering on the edge of an unknown abyss. I could slip at any time. Would falling be a good thing? I didn't want to crush on her. I was twenty-seven years old.

My office phone rang and I answered without even looking down at the display. "Lily Croft."

"Hope D'Marco."

I gasped and sat up straight in my chair. "Hope. Hi." I had no idea what to say to her other than hi, which I said a few times in a row. *Settle down, Lily.*

"Next Friday is the monthly concert, and I wanted to invite you to it. Maybe this time you can stay a little bit longer."

"How did you get my number?" I asked. My lack of filter with Hope was ridiculous.

"When we had dinner the other night, you said you worked at B and T, and I looked it up. I hope you don't mind. I gave you my number, but you haven't called me yet," she said.

I heard her smile through the phone. She was teasing me. I gripped the receiver harder and tried to sound like a normal person. "I didn't think you really wanted me to call you," I said. Normal people said that, right?

"I wouldn't have given you my number otherwise. So, what do you say? Will you attend? I'll save the seat in the very back row, closest to the door for you."

I couldn't tell if she was joking or being serious. "Um, yes. I'll attend." I knew I was going to be a wreck. Seven days to think about it.

"Great. Hopefully I'll see you before then, but if I don't, would you like to do dinner after that? We don't have to go anywhere. I can cook us something instead. My place isn't too far away."

I stood up. Did Hope just ask me out on a date or was this a friendship thing? I started pacing, but my steps were severely limited by a short phone cord. I was sure I looked crazy to anybody watching me. "Sure. That sounds great. Next Friday is my last day here, so I might get out early."

"That's even better. You can help us set up. I'm not going to lie, though, I'll miss you lingering out front."

I was quiet for a few seconds because I wasn't sure how to process that. Was she teasing me or had I actually become a stalker?

"Hey, I'm kidding. I love that you enjoy listening. I just wish you were going to be around longer. Your advice is immeasurable."

"I'm sorry about that. I should have done a better job of explaining myself." I cringed recalling my direct advice. Hope had been nothing but sweet and kind and I'd been such a jerk. I had a week to read up on interacting with people, specifically beautiful ones who made my heart beat faster and made me sweat like a teenager. If I wanted any kind of meaningful relationship with her, I was going to have to do a better job communicating.

"Will I see you before then?"

I gulped. Did she just ask me out again? How could one phone call result in two dates?

"This weekend is going to be nice and I thought maybe we could go do something fun outside. There are a few outdoor events, or we could go to the Lincoln Park Conservatory. Their flowers are in full bloom and it's nice and relaxing."

"Yes. That sounds nice." I finally sat down. This was going to happen. I wanted it to and she was trying. It was time to take a deep breath, count to ten, and submit.

"Great. Would you like to meet there? At noon tomorrow? I'll bring lunch," she said.

"I'll bring dessert, then." I couldn't show up empty-handed.

"You bring a blanket for us to sit on. Leave all the food to me."

"Okay." I was so nervous and stressed that I hung up and forgot to say good-bye. I held my head in my hands and groaned. How was I so bad at this?

❖

I saw Hope across the fountain and watched her for a few moments before I walked to her. My heart drummed against my chest, the beat fast and furious, and I took several deep breaths to calm down. She was wearing capris, a thin scoop-neck T-shirt, and flats. Her hair was pulled back, too, and I smiled when she looked down at her wrist for the time. She was thinking about her grandfather. Realizing that I was close to being late, I stepped away from my hiding place.

"You look great," she said when she saw me.

I looked down at my summer dress and sandals. My hair was pulled back and out of my face. "Thank you. So do you." She really did. I offered to carry the basket for her, but she waved me off.

"It's pretty heavy," she said.

"Did you just call me a wimp?" I asked.

She smiled at me. "I believe that you, Ms. Lily Croft, just made your first joke with me, and that makes me happy," she said. At least I knew she was here because of me. Me. No other reason. She was willing to give me a chance at something. "And no, I just have it perfectly balanced on my arm like Little Red Riding Hood. I scoped out the area and found a really nice place over there." She pointed over to an area far enough from the roses so that the bees wouldn't bother us, but close enough that we could enjoy the fragrance of them. We had the shade of a Japanese maple tree so the sun wasn't so hot. It was perfect. I wiped my hands across my dress several times before I felt Hope's fingers still me. "There's no reason to be nervous. It's just me." Her eyes were so trustworthy that I forced myself to relax. I counted to ten slowly before I responded.

"It's because it's you," I said honestly.

"Well, then it's the good kind of nerves. At least it is for me," she said and pulled her hand back. "Now let me show you what we have." Hope pulled out different containers of pasta salad, fruit salad, bread, and a tiny bottle of wine. "I know you drink beer, so I hope you are okay with wine. It's red, so it's not too sweet."

"Confession time," I said. Hope stopped and gave me her undivided attention, which unnerved me and excited me at the same time. I fidgeted with the hem of my dress. "I can count on one hand how many alcoholic drinks I've had in my life."

"We don't have to drink anything at all. I also have water." She was so sweet.

"I'm sure you know this already, but, well, I'm kind of a mess." My nervous smile couldn't find a place to land, so it went from one corner of my mouth to the other until I gave up and shrugged at her.

"I don't think you're a mess at all. I think you are a very shy, beautiful woman who doesn't like a lot of attention. I completely understand. All big thinkers are one step ahead of the rest of us."

She busied herself by fixing plates. I tried hard not to stare at her but was failing miserably. Hope said I was beautiful. I was plain. I wore very little makeup, my hair had zero style even though it was long and wavy, and my clothes were plain. I smoothed down the tiny hairs I felt curl out from the back of my neck. Being this close to her made me even more nervous, so I started the list in my head. Deep breaths. Count to ten.

"Close your eyes."

I turned and looked at her. "What?"

"Close your eyes. Trust me." My eyelids fluttered shut and I took a deep breath. The walls that were tight around my heart started to wobble. This woman was getting through to me in just a few short weeks. "Okay, tell me what you hear."

I lifted my eyebrows in surprise. She was playing my game. I took a deep breath and held it before I answered.

"I hear birds singing, which is a nice change from the pigeons that coo on the windowsills. There are children laughing nearby, possibly playing a game of hide-and-seek. I hear the chain links on the swings creak with the breeze. Every few seconds the wind picks up and twirls the leaves. That sound makes me the happiest."

"Because it's a relaxing and calming noise. What else do you hear?" Her hand touched mine. The struggle to pull away from her touch and the desire to lean into it was real. I concentrated hard to answer her.

"I hear you. You're humming. It's so low and sweet." I opened my eyes and looked at her. "Or maybe I can hear you through your touch. Does that make sense?"

"Completely. You definitely listen better than most people do. That's why I trust what you tell me about my playing and getting the pauses right. Your sensitivity to sound is a gift. Thank you for sharing it with me."

I sighed when she pulled her hand away. I wanted to tell her why I listened, but I wasn't ready. Jillian Crest was a lifetime ago. One I didn't want to revisit on a date. "Have any more kids signed up for lessons? How's the organization going?" It was a safe topic.

"Eh, we are kind of struggling. It's hard to get the kids in that location. We are hoping to generate more attention via social media, and we've visited nearby schools. Some counselors still believe in music programs. I guess it's just a matter of time." Hope furrowed her eyebrows.

"I'm sure it will pick up. At least half of all adults played an instrument growing up. Once they realize it's free and available for their children, then maybe there will be more attendance. What about a flyer sent home or however parents get information? Email?"

"That's a great idea. Instead of the counselors, maybe I should talk to the principals and vice principals," she said. I liked the way she nibbled at her bread while she was deep in thought. We were sitting close enough that I could reach over and wipe the errant crumb off her upper lip, but I didn't have the nerve. I was just getting comfortable sharing a blanket with her. I couldn't imagine reaching out and touching her, especially her full, beautiful lips. Hope would run away screaming. Or would she? My adrenaline at the prospect of Hope kissing me made me stand.

"Do you want to go for a walk?" I looked down at Hope, who was completely relaxed on the blanket. The food was still unpacked and half of her lunch still on her plate. "I'm sorry. That was rude." I sat back down.

"Don't be silly. That's fine. Let me just clear up this stuff. It'll just take a minute." She didn't seem bothered by my request.

"Why are you so agreeable with me?" I blurted out.

She didn't hesitate. "Because I like you and I want to get to know you. I know you are skittish around me and I think it's because you like me, too. I find you refreshing. You are pure and sweet, even if you struggle with communicating." She was direct, but I suddenly needed her to know everything about me, well, except the whole music thing.

"I'm bad at this. I don't know how to read people. I've never had a girlfriend or a best friend before. I'm more awkward than you think I am." I looked down at the blanket and started playing with a piece of grass that had blown onto it. Did I really just confess all of that out loud to the one person I actually liked? I groaned.

"Hey, I don't care about that. It's just us here." She touched my arm again, but this time I felt a slight shake in her fingers. Great. I just scared her off. I watched as she rubbed her thumb across my forearm a few times. "Lily." I looked up at her. "We are just two people enjoying a Saturday afternoon at the park. I have no expectations other than to see you break out of your shell a bit more. I already worked one joke out of you. I wonder how many more I'll hear before this date ends."

We really were on a date. I smiled at the fluttering butterflies inside my body, thinking I would float away if my hands weren't clutching the blanket, tightly holding me in place.

CHAPTER SEVEN

It was an actual date, Clio. She said it." I picked him up and swung him around high up above my head. He wasn't amused. As a matter of fact, I wasn't sure I'd ever seen that look of disdain on his face before. I felt a rumbling against my thumbs and figured he was two seconds away from scratching the shit out of me, so I carefully dropped him on the couch. He bolted. "Yeah, sorry, big guy. I got a little carried away."

When Hope walked me to the train station, I'd been a complete mess. Was I supposed to kiss her? Were we supposed to make plans? Did I completely blow my chances with her? When my train showed up, she gave me a quick hug and I felt her lips brush across my cheek when she pulled away. I almost melted right there. She said she would text me later.

"How is somebody so perfect as Hope D'Marco interested in me, Clio?" I asked an empty room.

My phone buzzed on the table. *Did you make it home safely?*

I held my breath and froze. It was Hope.

I did. Thank you for checking on me. The good news about texting was that I had time to filter what I said. Maybe texting was the ideal form of communication for me. *I had fun today. Thanks for the invite.* I deleted the second "thank you" and opted for the more casual "thanks." I'd already confessed I was awkward. I didn't want her to think I was a complete freak.

How's Clio?

He's mad at me so he's hiding. I didn't want to tell her the reason why, so I kept it vague.

Oh, no. What did you do? So much for keeping it vague.

I hugged him a little too hard when I got home. I forget he's not a stuffed animal sometimes. I swiped through the photos on my camera and sent her one of Clio.

He's gorgeous. I can't wait to meet him. She punctuated it with a smiley face that mirrored my own. She was still interested.

Dinner at my place next week? I sent it before I had a chance to think. It was just like the piano app on my phone. I acted before I thought. I waited.

Only if it's a little bit later. With the concert this week, I have extra practices with students. Can we do dinner around eight? Or is that too late?

She could have said midnight and I would have pretended that was perfect for me. *That's fine. Or we can wait until after the concert and do it next week.* Self-sabotage. I was great at it.

How about Tuesday? Just text me your address and I'll see you and Clio at eight. I'll bring dessert. I texted her my address and looked around my place. It was always clean, but my energy level ramped up the second she said yes. I mentally made a plan to clean all day Sunday. I also didn't want her to have an allergy fit, so I would vacuum again right before she showed up. Right then, I was going to the gym to work off my excess energy and try not to think about Hope being the first person I'd ever invited over to my place.

❖

"So, this is your last week?" Mr. Hoyt knocked and walked into my office. I looked up from the computer and pulled out my earbuds. I was listening to a book on how to be social without sounding like an idiot or something like that. It was Tuesday, and Hope was coming over for dinner. My house was spotless. I wasn't even going to try to cook. I was too nervous and I knew I would burn myself or the food. I had the Italian restaurant across the street on speed dial. Their Caprese salad and bruschetta was a nice, light meal that I knew Hope would enjoy.

"Yes. I will be out of your hair in no time." I tried hard not to look at his shiny, balding head that seemed to perpetually sweat. Fuck, I needed a filter. There were about three seconds of awkwardness as we both mentally maneuvered past it.

"You know, if you ever want to transfer here, we would love to have you full-time. With our company growing as much as it is, we could use the help on a permanent basis," he said.

"That's a very generous suggestion." I was noncommittal. I liked working at B&T, but I missed working from home and hanging out with Clio more. Socializing myself was only going to happen taking baby steps. My confidence was twice what it was, but I was not ready to spend every day with people. "I really enjoyed my time here, but I also like my job at Banks Corporation."

He nodded. "I understand. Just keep me in mind if you are ever looking." He smiled and shuffled backward out of my office.

Nice guy, but really weird. I put my headphones on and

continued listening to a woman tell me that I was important. She suggested ways to avoid social awkwardness. Sometimes people didn't get along. Sometimes they did, but it was hard to read between the lines. I was bound and determined to remain calm. I nixed medication a long time ago. I didn't need any since I worked from home and was rarely around people. I looked at the clock. It was only two. It was time for a break and I knew exactly where I was headed.

I smiled when I heard the music. Somebody was jazzing it up with a trumpet. A few minutes later, a percussion joined in. I heard the mess-ups and the laughter associated with them, still foreign to me. I was tense but reminded myself to relax. They were having a good time upstairs, so I should enjoy it, too. I sat down on the steps, closed my eyes, and listened to the music. I didn't care who was watching me. I wanted to be a part of this fun. Hope wasn't instructing, and I wondered if she was inside with another student in a different room.

"Hi, you." As if she read my mind, Hope bounced down the stairs and sat down next to me. She placed her hand on my knee and leaned into me. "What a nice surprise."

I clenched my hands into fists to keep from shaking. The nearness of her was a lot to absorb. It was great, but also unnerving. She must have sensed my apprehension because she scooted a few inches away from me. The smile never left her face.

"I needed a break and thought this was the perfect way to escape," I said.

"Well, it's a nice surprise. I didn't think I would see you until tonight." I noticed a sprinkle of freckles across the bridge of her nose and wondered if our excursion Saturday brought them out. I looked up when the trumpet slid into a soft and slow soulful song. It was beautiful. We both clapped when the student was done.

"That was great. Who's playing?" Not that I would know the student, but I had to know their name. Plus, I was so nervous with Hope so close to me and had energy to expel.

"Tyler. You probably haven't heard him before. He's sixteen and just started coming here for lessons. This kid doesn't need lessons. He just needs to be heard. He will definitely play on Friday," she said. She was proud of him.

"How long is the concert?" I asked. Since I'd left early last month, I wasn't sure.

"About an hour and a half. Wait, are you bailing on me already?" She smiled.

"No, not at all. I was curious because I left early last time. I'm going to try really hard to stay until the end." She didn't question me. For whatever reason, Hope let me be me. She never pressed me for information. She was the perfect person to bring me out of my shell.

"You probably need to get back to it. Long day ahead." I thumbed behind me and Hope's shoulders slumped.

"Yeah, I know, but I wanted to at least say hi. Hi." She was so cute right now, and so close.

"Hi. I should probably go, too," I said. She stood and reached her hand out to help me up. Without thinking, I slid my hand into hers and almost moaned at her warmth and strength. She pulled me up and stepped closer so we were only a few inches apart. I gasped at her nearness.

"Have a good day, Lily. I'll see you tonight at eight." Gone was the playful Hope. She'd been replaced by a very sensual one. Her voice got a tinge huskier and her eyes narrowed.

I swallowed. I walked away frightened and exhilarated for tonight.

CHAPTER EIGHT

C lio, I need you around, especially if I run out of things to talk about."

I had brushed him a thousand times until his fur was shiny and he was pissed off. You could take the cat out of the alley, but not the alley out of the cat. He didn't like pampering at all. Food, a warm bed, and an occasional full body pat from right behind his crooked ears to his misshapen tail. That was it. That was all he wanted.

I glanced at the clock for the fifth time in the last two minutes. Hope was supposed to be here in ten minutes. The food was on its way over and my house was in tip-top shape. There wasn't a speck of dirt or a loose Clio hair anywhere to be found. I looked around. My place was practical but not cozy. The soft gray couch was comfortable but plain. I had zero flair. The only colorful thing in my living room was a red umbrella I had hanging from the coat rack by the front door. I regretted not having artwork on the walls, but it was too late to do anything about it. The doorbell rang and I buzzed up the food. I tipped Ryan, the nice college kid who delivered, and shoved him quickly out into the hall. Not that I wanted Hope to think I cooked the food, but I was nervous and needed a few minutes to breathe.

My phone rang. "Hi, it's me. I'm downstairs."

I buzzed Hope up and paced until I heard a firm, yet friendly knock at the door.

"Wish me luck, Clio." He looked at me curiously but didn't move from his perch on the armrest of the sofa.

"You made it," I all but whispered to Hope. She wore jeans and a cute blouse, and I wondered if she went home to change or brought the clothes to work and changed. My mind was obsessing about her wardrobe. Be normal, I mentally scolded myself.

"Of course I did. I wouldn't miss this for anything," she said. Oh, boy. She was giving me the same look that she did on the stairs earlier today.

"You changed." Apparently I wasn't going to let it go.

"So did you," she said. "Are you going to invite me in?"

"Oh, my gosh. Yes, please. Come in." I stepped back to let her in. I smiled at the floral perfume I now recognized as her scent.

"You must be Clio." She reached into her purse and pulled out a tiny toy mouse and dangled it in front of his nose. He studied her, then the toy, then her again. She shook it faster. "Get it, boy, get it." He lazily reached up and pulled it from her grip.

We both watched as he tucked it under his hindquarters. He returned our stares and yawned.

"I have no explanation for his actions, but thank you for thinking of him." Great. My cat was also a weirdo. I was really banking on his normalcy to keep us going through the evening.

Hope laughed. "Cats are like kids. Completely unpredictable and adorable at the same time." She rubbed his head and jawline and took a moment to look around my condo. "You have a very nice place."

"Thank you," I said. My entire nonexistent childhood paid

for it, I thought. I gave her a quick tour but stayed completely away from my bedroom. It was more of a point and explain thing because I was worried about the food getting cold.

"I love that you can see the fire escape from your living room. It gives the place such character."

"Right there is where Clio stood. He just stared at me and meowed. I never had any pets before, so it was quite the experience. He was wary of me and me of him for several days. Now he lets me hold him and swing him around," I said.

"Except he doesn't like it when you do that," Hope said.

I smiled recalling our text messages from the other night. "True. If you are hungry, let's eat before the food gets cold. They just delivered it from across the street."

Hope had brought over wine and she poured herself a glass. When I poured myself one, too, I saw the look of surprise on her face before she covered it up. I needed all the help I could get. We fixed our plates and I followed Hope into the formal dining room. It felt snobbish to sit here, but the view of the city was nice. I never ate in this room. It reminded me too much of my upbringing, but I sat down and focused on Hope, not on my past.

"It smells delicious," she said.

"I don't cook." I was so nervous that I was resorting back to my Neanderthal grunts and reminded myself to relax. I took a deep breath and explained. "I mean, it's hard to cook for one person, so I never developed a passion for it like so many people." I cooked breakfast like a champ, but inviting a woman back to your place for bacon and eggs just seemed too comfortable and plain.

"I love to cook, but you're right. It's hard to cook for one person. My refrigerator contents consist of yogurts, vegetables, jellies I don't remember buying, and beer I forget to drink," she said.

I took a sip of wine. "So, why are you only cooking for one person? How is somebody so accomplished still single?" I asked. I stopped myself from bestowing compliment after compliment: you're so beautiful, you're so sweet and nice, you do such great work for the community. Asking why she was single was a giant step for my comfort level. I took another drink. Red wine wasn't bad when washed down with Italian food.

"I just needed to focus on me. My last relationship suffered because I was so involved in getting Leading Note up and running that my girlfriend faded away. I forgot that I was part of something greater than myself." She shrugged, took a bite of food, and continued after swallowing. "Now that things are relaxed, sort of, at the organization, I decided to get back to me."

"What happened to your ex-girlfriend? Did you try reaching out to her?" I was so curious that I didn't even think that the questions might be hurtful. "I'm sorry. You don't have to answer that."

"She moved on, and rightfully so. I harbor no ill will toward her. I see her at functions here and there." She pulled a piece of mozzarella from her salad and held it down for Clio.

"He will sniff that forever and never eat…" I stopped talking when Clio leaned up, delicately took the cheese from Hope's fingers, and chewed it up. He looked back up at her when he was done. "I can't believe that. Cheese is the only thing he won't eat. At least not from me."

"He knows good food. Perhaps you should spoil him more." She winked at me to let me know she was kidding when she saw my chest puff up as I started to defend myself. Hope had a way of putting me at ease, something several of my many therapists couldn't do.

We moved our conversation from the dining room into the

living room and stared out at the city. Hope asked me about my job, what I loved about Chicago, and I asked her about music. It felt safe talking about it with her. I trusted her. She didn't push me, didn't ask me my background.

"Close your eyes," she said. I smiled and obliged. "Tell me what you hear."

"I hear the heart of the city. Beating. Making music." I opened my eyes and looked at her. She shook her head.

"That's not good enough. Close your eyes and listen, really listen. Tell me the city's song," she said.

I did as she asked and focused on the little noises. "The constant whirls of the air conditioners, the moaning and hissing of the buses, the continuous *thump thump* as people drive over the manhole covers." I stopped and listened even harder. "I think I even hear a trumpet somewhere." I smiled and opened my eyes to find Hope only a few inches from my face. I stilled and held my breath. She placed a tiny kiss on the corner of my mouth.

"Is this okay?" she whispered against my skin.

I nodded. Excitement and fear coursed through my veins when I felt her lips very softly, very slowly, press against mine. Our first kiss was the purest thing I'd ever felt. It stripped me of every thought, every nerve, every hesitation I had about her. When our lips moved together in a rhythm that came to me as naturally as breathing, my whole being exploded with a melody I had never heard or felt before. She left me breathless with the softest kiss.

She slowly pulled away from me, her warm fingers touching my neck. "Wow."

I stared at her. I was sure every emotion flashed across my face from disbelief to happiness to utter shock. I'd been kissed by three women in my life. Carrie, in college, who tried to have sex with me every single time we were alone, but never got anywhere. Gina, a woman I met online, who slobber-kissed me good night after a lukewarm date. And Hope, who created the magic that just happened. I didn't know how to process my feelings, so I stared. Was this how it was for everybody? I'd felt the world instantly stop once before, and my life changed forever. I'd just felt it stop again, and I knew my life had changed again. This time, it changed for the better. The corners of my mouth curled up.

"Yeah, wow." There were no words for this moment.

She reached out for my hand and stroked the top of my fingers. "That was really nice. Thank you." She was thanking me? I didn't understand.

"Um, why?" Ah, yes, my vast vocabulary that I reserved for Hope just pushed its way out. "I mean, you don't have to thank you—I mean, thank me." I was a wreck. I wanted to bury my embarrassed face in my hands and hide. I refrained and instead looked down at my hands resting in my lap.

"Because you trusted me close to you." She interlocked her fingers with mine. "You're shaking."

"This…" I paused because my voice shook. I cleared my throat. "This is very new to me and I like it. I just don't know what to do."

"Hey. Stop. Look at me," Hope said. I looked at her. She brushed my hair out of my face with her fingertips and tucked it behind my ear. "There is no right or wrong here. We are just two women hopefully starting a relationship. I'm in no rush and I'm not going anywhere. Okay?" I nodded. "I know you're nervous. I am, too, but I'm also excited to get to know you better. So, if you're interested in me and want to see where this goes, I'm willing to try."

I nodded again. "Okay." I was quietly processing everything.

"Okay." She sat next to me and quietly held my hand until

I relaxed and got comfortable with her nearness and warmth. "Tell me what you do when you aren't working. I don't want to say what do you do for fun, but what keeps you busy and out of trouble?"

I laughed. I'd never been in trouble. "I like to play the stock market, but that doesn't really keep me out of trouble."

"Another joke. I love it," Hope said.

I smiled. "I like shooting pool and playing table tennis. And I do read a lot. What about you? What do you like to do?"

"I love to bake. I also like to read. I'm horrible at pool and I've never tried table tennis. I like spending time with my family. They're loud and obnoxious, but they are a part of me. I don't have a lot of spare time, but when I do, I try to learn different instruments."

I felt a slight squeeze when she talked about her family. I knew that if I met them, it couldn't all be at once. Based on the stories she'd told me, I couldn't imagine being in a large, loud crowd without freaking out a few times.

"I also have a confession," Hope said.

My heart sped up, then felt like it stopped. I was nervous for what she was going to say, for no other reason than I'd learned to always expect the worst. "I hate finances and everything to do with math. I don't know a single thing about them. You said stock market and I went blank. My eyes glossed over. My brain turned to jelly." She nudged her shoulder into mine as I relaxed. Her confession was playful.

"It's not for everyone."

"Why do you like math so much?"

She was genuinely interested and I told myself to keep my answer short and sweet so that she wouldn't keel over from boredom. "I like it because it's definite. It's not going to surprise me." Simple. I nodded at her.

"I can respect that. I could never make a living out of it,

but I can understand how it appeals to some people. And by some people, I mean smart people."

"I'm not that smart," I said. I was, but I didn't want to come across as pompous, so I kept quiet.

"Where did you go to school?" She shifted on the couch so that she was facing me.

"Um, I went to Princeton," I said.

"How did you end up in Chicago?" She reached for her almost empty wineglass. I refilled it, and topped off my glass to make it fair. The first glass had relaxed me. Maybe the second glass would stop me from shaking at her nearness.

"Word of mouth, actually. One of my instructors at the university was related to Jason Banks and recommended me for a position there. It's really the only job I've had since graduating." I leaned back and tried to relax. I wanted Hope to hold my hand again but I didn't want to ask, and I certainly didn't feel comfortable reaching out for hers.

"I almost failed algebra," Hope said. We both laughed. "I had the worst instructor ever. Even if I had an inkling of understanding it, he squelched my need for more." Hope shook her head at her memory.

"I love it so much, but there was no way I could ever be an instructor. I'm horrible in front of a crowd. I even have a problem just talking to one person."

Hope reached out for my hand. "You're doing fine. I'm having a good time with you." She looked at her watch and sat up. "Oh, my gosh. It's so late. I really hate to do this, but I have to go. This is my hell week and I'm needing to get some sleep." She pouted at me, indicating she didn't want to leave.

I didn't want her to leave either, but I stood up and walked with her to the door. The quivers in my stomach fluttered up and down my body the closer we got to saying good-bye.

She reached down for my hand again. "Thank you very

much for tonight. The food was great, but the company even better." She leaned forward and kissed me softly.

I didn't know if I was kissing her right, but I knew she liked it because she moved closer to me until our bodies touched. I felt the soft tip of her tongue stroke my lips, and I opened my mouth to kiss her back as decadently as she was kissing me. I moaned when I felt her body next to mine. I couldn't help it. I felt her hands slide up my back to wind in my hair. She took complete control of me and I loved it.

"Thanks for coming over. Let me know when you make it home safely," I said. My insides churned with nervous energy, but my voice was calm as if Hope kissing me was as normal as breathing. She answered with a sweet smile. I almost reached out to touch her face, but I stopped myself. I didn't know how to be romantic and I didn't want to act on my impulses like a teenager, so I just stood there. She kissed me again and slipped quietly through the door. I closed it and leaned up against it.

"We did it, Clio. Thanks for helping me." I headed over to him, but he scampered off, knowing full well he was in for another swing around the room and clearly not wanting any part of it.

CHAPTER NINE

So how was it?" Hope greeted me with a smile that almost
made me crumple to the floor. It was flirty and sexy and
made my knees weak. The last time I saw her, her body was
pressed against me and her mouth was slowly seducing mine.
I liked kissing Hope. A lot.

"It was nice. I liked the people I worked with there. At
least the ones I talked to," I said. Hope stayed in my personal
space, and even though I felt skittish, I didn't back away. I
wanted her next to me. It was just going to take time for me
to get used to her closeness. We were alone in the foyer. She
ran the pad of her thumb softly on my bottom lip and I stopped
talking.

"Can I kiss you?" she whispered.

I nodded.

She leaned into me, her right hand above my hip, her left
hand cupping my cheek. It was a swift and sweet kiss, but it
packed a punch that had me breathless.

"I really like kissing you," I said.

"I really like kissing you, too." She took a step back, ran
her hand down my arm, and laced her fingers with mine. The
chills quickly followed the path of her fingers and I shivered.
She smiled. She clearly knew what her touch did to me. "Come

on, I'm going to put you to work. We can put your things in my office."

I followed her up to the third floor and into her modest office. It held few personal items. She noticed my reaction.

"Yeah, I know. I need to make it more inviting. I think you are the only person who has been in my office aside from the staff."

"You haven't been here that long, though. It takes time." I thought about my bare walls at home. Sometimes it takes years. Hope didn't strike me as the kind of woman who would take that long, though. She wasn't broken. She welcomed color and fun things.

"I should make the effort, though. Anyway, what can I make you do?" She looked at me innocently, but winked.

I blushed and nervously played with the collar of my blouse. "Ah, anything really. I can help set up chairs, decorate the hall, put food out," I stammered. Her flirtatious manner threw me, but in a good way. I wanted her attention.

"Let's decorate. I can always use help." She handed me a bag of various items I wasn't sure what to do with.

I looked down at my outfit. I should have brought a change of clothes with me. At least I was wearing slacks. My blouse was kind of tight, but not too restrictive. I wanted to look good for Hope, so I took my time getting ready and an even longer time freshening up before I arrived. B&T said good-bye to me, but I didn't leave the building until twenty minutes later. I slinked out, hoping nobody would see me.

I followed her down to the foyer where we hung paper streamers and tiny white lights encased in paper lanterns of all different colors. They added a welcoming flair to the entrance. I liked the blue ones the best and decided it was the perfect accent color for my living room.

"I think we did a good job." Hope stood back and admired our work.

"Miss D'Marco. Can we practice a bit before tonight?" Tony walked in, clarinet in hand. His excitement was evident by the ear-to-ear smile and his small dance when she nodded at him.

Hope turned to me. "I'm sorry. If you want, you can wait in the concert hall, or up in my office while we practice. Or just walk around and do whatever," she said.

"I can loiter, if you don't mind."

"Loiter away," she said and followed Tony into a room.

I hung out in the foyer because I wasn't sure what rooms were occupied and which ones weren't. I wasn't comfortable enough peeking in the windows either. I sat on a brown leather wingback chair and picked up this week's *Masters of Music* magazine. I was completely out of the loop on the latest anything. I wasn't sure who was still performing or who was the next best thing. I put the magazine back down.

"Oh, Lily. Can you help me?" Agnes came over to me waving her cell phone. "I need your help. Can you please sit with Kylie for a minute while I take this call? It's really important," she whispered.

I looked at her as fear coursed through my body. What did she need me to do? I automatically nodded and stood up. "What?" I was confused.

She grabbed my hand and dragged me into one of the therapy rooms.

"Just keep an eye on Kylie. She's one of our music therapy students. I'll be back in two minutes." She disappeared, quietly closing the door on her way out.

Kylie, a cute little girl who looked to be about eight or nine years old, sat next to a standard Yamaha upright that you could find at any music school. The piano wasn't much to look at but produced a decent sound from what I remembered. I tentatively introduced myself to Kylie because I had no idea what else to do. She was so focused on the piano that my introduction did nothing to distract her. I walked over to the piano and stared at it, too. We both probably had different reasons for our infatuations.

"Kylie, what do you like to hear?" I was sure her answer was "anything," but I stared at the keys waiting for my internal battle to work itself out. I needed to do this for Kylie, but I really needed to do this for myself. I brushed my fingertips over the keys but didn't press down. The smoothness of the keys made the corners of my mouth twitch in recognition. I didn't know if it was happiness I felt, or resolution. I wanted to play. I wanted to create something. Kylie made a noise at me.

"You want me to play?" I asked. She smiled, or maybe was always smiling and I just noticed. I took a deep breath and hit a key. The sound resonated around me, inside me, but didn't break me. I hit a second key. Then I played a few notes. I felt my heart race inside my chest, chasing the demons out, and played an entire scale without even thinking about it.

Kylie laughed.

"Did you like that?" I asked. I wasn't brave enough to sit on the bench, so I hunched over and played "Twinkle, Twinkle, Little Star" before I took a step back from the piano. I took a deep breath again and looked at Kylie. The smile on her face couldn't have been any larger. Her reaction made me smile. For just a moment, it gave me peace.

"Thank you so much for watching Kylie." Agnes busted in the door, her voice breathless and rushed.

"It was no problem." I nervously tucked my hair behind my ear and excused myself.

"You can stay if you want," she said. I waved her off and headed for the door.

Once it was safely shut behind me, I smiled. I did it. I didn't let the fear of the piano get to me. And I made Kylie smile. She was genuinely happy about the quick, simple song I played, and so was I. It wasn't anything profound, but it was life changing. I sat back in the wingback chair and waited for Hope. I wished I could share this momentous occasion with her, but she didn't know my struggles. Only Dr. Monroe knew, and she was probably unavailable. I would email her later. I stood because I was too excited to sit, but had nowhere to go so I sat again. It was close to five and the concert began at six. Why did I show up so early? A vision of Hope popped into my head and I smiled. I was here because I wanted to impress a girl. I stood again when two people walked into the foyer.

"Do you work here?" the woman asked. I panicked and shook my head at her. "Oh, I'm sorry. We are here to pick up our daughter Kylie."

My eyes lit up at her name. "She's with Agnes in room B." I pointed behind me.

They nodded and sat on the couch. For fear of looking like a total freak, I sat back down and waited with them.

"Do you have a child here?"

I didn't want to have a conversation, but I had to be polite for Hope's sake. "No. I'm just here for the concert. I'm friends with Hope." I nervously traced my finger along the small cracks in the arm of the leather chair, desperately wanting to avoid a conversation with Kylie's parents.

"Oh, Paul. We should stay for it. Kylie would love it," she said. Paul grunted something noncommittal. His body language reminded me of every person who was dragged to my concerts and didn't want to be there.

"You know." My voice squeaked. I cleared my throat and started again. "You know, I saw how excited Kylie was when Agnes played the piano. I think a concert would make her happy." I felt tiny beads of sweat pop out on my temples. I was injecting myself where I didn't belong. "And it would be so great for the kids to have a bigger audience."

"Settled. We're staying."

I avoided eye contact with Paul.

"What about dinner?" he asked.

Again, I couldn't help myself. "I know they are going to have snack-type foods out here in a bit. Plus, there's a little diner only a few blocks from here that serves great comfort food." My voice trailed off when I did look at Paul. He wasn't impressed with my suggestion.

"Oh, we didn't have anything else planned. We can nibble for a bit and then leave the concert early if Kylie gets fussy," she said. More like if Paul gets fussy, I thought. I smiled at her in approval. At least Kylie was going to hear more music.

"Here we are." Agnes pushed Kylie's wheelchair through the door. Kylie's smile lit her entire face, and by the time she reached us, we were all smiling along with her. "We really enjoyed today's session."

"Did you have fun?" Kylie's mom stood and leaned over to kiss her daughter.

It was apparent that music had lifted Kylie's spirits. I felt another shift inside. Tiny, but enough of one to make me notice. Or maybe it was a spark. Kylie looked right at me, and for a few seconds, I felt like I was responsible for her happiness. When I played before, it was for an entire audience and not for just one person. Kylie's reaction was so precious, I was sure I could do it again. Maybe, just maybe, I could ease back into the piano one note at a time, one person at a time.

CHAPTER TEN

T hank you all for showing up and your generous donations," Hope said after applauding all of the children who bowed to their audience.

I'd stayed the entire time. I was drenched in sweat and afraid to leave my seat, but I'd survived all of it. The hardest was when Hope played. I was on edge and trying hard not to mentally critique her. She only messed up once on that same damn transition as before. Our eyes briefly met when that happened. I saw her shoulders sag for just a moment when she realized she waited too long. I applauded a little harder when she and Tony were done because I knew she was beating herself up about it. I didn't move from my chair until most of the people cleared out.

"I know, I screwed up." Hope sat in the chair in front of me and turned her body so she could face me.

I reached out and put my hand on her forearm. "You were great. All the kids were wonderful. I'm glad I stayed the entire time." I smiled encouragingly at her. Her smile back didn't meet her eyes. "Seriously, you did a wonderful job. I've heard that piece a thousand times, and you still made my heart leap in my chest." The emotional response to music was a universal understanding among musicians. The fact that I said it to somebody I was interested in only made me sound desperate. Hope didn't know I was a musician. She thought I was a music aficionado. I had to backpedal to avoid sounding creepy. "I mean, you played it so well that I barely noticed your stutter." I wasn't going to pretend that I didn't hear it because I didn't want to lie to Hope, as hypocritical as that was.

"You're sweet to say that, but I get nervous with you in the room," she said.

I almost snorted. I shook my head at her. "You shouldn't be. You are a wonderful teacher to these kids and you know music better than most instructors." I looked down because I couldn't look into her brown eyes any longer. She was intense. And very close to me.

"Do you still want to have dinner? Go celebrate?"

"What are we celebrating?"

"We are celebrating the completion of your project, tonight's successful concert, and maybe we could celebrate us, too," she said.

I really wanted a hot shower, an ice-cold water, and to plop down on my couch. There was so much stimulation in my day that I felt overwhelmed. "Would you be upset with me if I wanted to go home? Today was just…" I paused because I didn't know how to tell her that it wasn't her, it was everything else. "Today was a lot for me to take. It was all good, just a little much."

The smile slid off her face and she nodded. "I understand."

"Let me help you clean up," I said and stood when she did.

"No, it's okay. It doesn't take long to clean up. The eight of us can knock this out in no time. Let's go get your stuff."

It was hard to keep up with her as she took the steps two at a time. I'd upset her and I didn't know how to make it right. This was all so new to me. Relationship rules. I didn't know them, only what I read about in books and saw in movies. She handed me my messenger bag and my purse. I reached out for them but stopped myself from taking them. I needed her to understand me, and if she was holding my stuff, she was less inclined to bolt.

"Hope. Stop. Can I please say what I need to?" I asked.

She took a deep breath and looked at me.

"I enjoy spending time with you. I loved the concert. It was incredible to see the children get so into the music and play. A lot happened to me today. I'm not used to attention at all. I'm not used to being around a lot of people, and I'm just drained." I was trying hard to keep it together, but how do you explain that you've been an isolated freak almost your entire life? "I know I can't explain my problems to you. They are mine and I need to deal with them. This is a big day for you, and you should go out and celebrate with everybody involved. I don't want to bring you down. I just want you to know that I'm thinking about you and I want to get to a place where being around a lot of people for a long period of time doesn't affect me as much as it does. It's just going to take time." I sniffed and blinked back my tears.

Hope leaned forward so that she was in my space. I didn't shrink back. "I'm sorry for being a baby about this. I just want to spend time with you. I know that this isn't easy and I should be more understanding," she said.

I smiled sadly, took the bags from her, and turned to leave when I felt her fingers slip into mine. She gently pulled me back around. This time, she didn't ask. Very slowly, she pressed her lips against mine. The tip of her tongue briefly touched my bottom lip as she softly sucked it into her mouth. I whimpered. She deepened the kiss and pressed her body into mine.

I stood there, bags in both hands, and tried hard to kiss her back. I wanted more. I dropped my bags and wrapped my arms around her, holding her in place. I heard a moan and almost smiled victoriously when I realized the sound was coming from her. I was doing something right. She ran her hands up and down my sides, and I felt my nipples harden when her fingers accidentally barely brushed the side of my breast. I wanted her to touch me, but I knew this wasn't the place for any of this.

"If you want to come over tonight, that would be nice," I said. Surprise registered in her eyes and I quickly explained myself. "I mean, this is nice, but not because of this. I just need to step away from everyone, but don't leave your celebration early."

She put her forehead against mine and sighed.

"Why don't you go home and relax? Get away from all of this. I know it's been a long day for you with your project ending and then having to sit here for several hours."

She was so understanding, but I still wanted to see her. "That would be great. Will you call me later?" That didn't sound too desperate.

"Definitely. Now get out of here before I lock this door and don't let you out."

I knew she was kidding, but I couldn't stop the shock from showing on my face. I was still new to all of this.

"Kidding. I'm just kidding. Sort of," she said.

❖

"Hi." Nobody called me except my boss, so I knew it was Hope. It was ten fifteen and I was on the couch with Clio, watching a cheesy romance movie and eating pizza. I'd checked my phone every two minutes until I finally gave up about ten minutes ago. Clio and I were thinking about retiring to the bedroom. The couch was nice, but not as comfortable as the bed.

"How are you? I've been worried about you." I heard the concern in her voice, and the fact that she cared warmed me.

"I'm better. My world is quiet now."

"You hung in there until the very end," she said. She understood me.

"It was really a nice concert. I loved listening to the kids. And Kylie stayed through most of it." They left about ten minutes before it was over. I counted that as a success.

"That's right. You watched Kylie for a few minutes while Agnes talked to her insurance agent. Thank you for helping."

"Kylie was so happy to hear music. She really loves the piano," I said.

"Did you play something for her?" Hope asked the question, dragging out every word as if she couldn't believe I did it.

"Sort of, but not really. I'm sure anybody could hit the keys and she would have enjoyed it." I fidgeted with Clio's collar. I was nervous that she would start asking more questions, the kind I didn't want to answer.

"Kylie truly appreciates music. Probably more so than most of our therapy children. She knows when something is good. Between you and her, I'll be playing perfectly soon." Hope laughed.

"I'm sorry about that. I really have no place giving you advice," I started to apologize again, but she stopped me.

"You've done nothing but help me. So stop it. I can handle constructive criticism." She was thankful, but I felt rude, especially the first time we talked. I cringed, recalling that conversation. I wasn't as rough around the edges with Hope anymore, but I was a far cry from being smooth. "Tell me about the rest of your night."

"I basically locked myself in, shut the world out, and cuddled with Clio, who is still perched on my chest." I rubbed his chin, which he jutted out at me and turned his head from side to side for thorough attention. We'd done this for hours before. "He's really good at calming me down."

"He's really sweet. I wish he liked me more," Hope said.

"Well, you'll need to come back over and visit him." Wow, that wasn't bad.

"Why don't we get together tomorrow? It's supposed to rain, but we could go see a movie or rent one."

I stiffened. "Um. Sure. We can rent a movie here. Maybe go out to dinner beforehand?"

I was already starting to get nervous. What if things got crazy? And by crazy, I meant what if she wanted more than kissing? I was just getting comfortable with her close to me, inside my personal space bubble. Visions of Carrie from college filled my head and I scowled at the memories. I knew Hope would be gentle with me. She asked if it was okay if she could kiss me. Did that even happen anymore? She was kind and thoughtful. She wasn't going to throw herself at me.

We made plans to meet at the Purple Pig for an early dinner. It was close to my place and would only be a quick cab ride back.

"I'm sorry I left early, but thank you for inviting me to the concert. It was great to hear the kids. And you."

"Thanks for coming. Good night, Lily." I was still smiling when I picked up Clio and dragged him off to bed thirty minutes later.

CHAPTER ELEVEN

I was early to everything. We agreed to meet at the Pig at five, but I showed up at four thirty. I had never eaten there and realized much too late why. Too many people. Even this early, the place was packed. I told myself to relax, that everything was fine. It was raining, so waiting for Hope outside wasn't an option. I leaned up against the wall near the hostess podium, my heart pounding rapidly in my chest. I closed my eyes and counted to ten.

"You know, there's a cute little sandwich shop down the block. Why don't we go there instead? Maybe take it back to your place?"

I opened my eyes to find Hope standing in front of me, blocking out the rest of the world. I nodded. She grabbed my hand and walked me outside. It wasn't raining too hard, but she opened her umbrella and tucked us underneath it.

"Hi." She handled the whole thing so amazingly well. My anxiety wasn't gone, but it was no longer controlling me.

"Hi, and thank you," I said.

She softly rubbed my arm out of comfort. Her touch was nice and her nearness even nicer. "Bad idea. I'd forgotten how crazy that place is."

She was so close to me that I could have kissed her if I

wanted to without much effort. I must have been staring at her lips because she stopped and I almost whacked my head on the front of the umbrella at my forward momentum.

"What is it?" I asked and looked around genuinely confused as to why we stopped in the middle of the sidewalk. It was crowded and people were scurrying around trying not to bump into us.

Hope leaned forward and kissed me. It wasn't gentle and sweet. It was more possessive, and passionate, and I had to clutch her elbow to keep myself upright.

"Nice. What was that for?" Did I really just ask her that?

"I liked the way you were looking at my mouth," she said, shrugging. "And you look really nice today and I wanted to say hello the right way."

"You say hello very well." My voice was shaky.

She playfully pulled me in the direction of the sandwich shop, which was thankfully not busy at all. It wasn't elegant, but smelled delicious, and I was ready for bread baked with rosemary and other spices.

"If you order a salad, I'm going to be upset." Hope leaned against me to see what I was looking at in the tri-folded paper menu on the countertop.

"You're not good for my diet."

Hope snorted and covered her mouth. "You do not need to diet." She looked me over. "You look beautiful." Heat raced up my body and flooded my neck and cheeks. "And now I've embarrassed you."

I reached up and rubbed my neck. I wanted to believe her, but I knew it wasn't true. I did, however, try a little harder before our date. I'd put on a touch of makeup and straightened my hair. The rain and humidity killed it within minutes, but there was a ghost of an attempt and I was glad it was noticed. A mirror behind the sandwich counter showed me a girl with rosy cheeks, bright eyes, and hair that didn't look half bad. Not beautiful, but definitely lively.

"Come on. Let's order so we can go relax and play with Clio." Hope knew exactly what to say.

I cleared my throat and placed my order after she did. She added chips and brownies to our order even though I protested.

"Let's just take a cab back," I said. The train would have taken forever and I was done being around people and standing in the rain.

"Agreed. Wait here. I'll get us one." She shook open the umbrella and stood on the side of the street for about ten seconds, holding her hand up for attention. She waved me over as the driver pulled to the curb.

I climbed in and gave him my address. We settled in for the short ride. Hope reached out for my hand. Her hands were cool from the rain, so I automatically rubbed them with mine without thinking of the intimacy of the act. My body was always warm, especially when I was tired. Today, it was because she was so close to me.

"Our backup plan isn't so bad," Hope said.

"I don't think so either. Thanks for accommodating me." I didn't need to say for what. We both knew I had issues being in crowded places. "It's not really fair to you though. I'm sure the Pig is a great restaurant."

Hope shrugged. "It's okay. I'd much rather spend time with you than the fifty people we would have sat by in that restaurant." I smiled at that. She nudged my shoulder. "You have a very nice smile."

Several years of orthodontics had ensured it was perfect. My parents needed their child to be all-around perfect—not just with musical instruments. "Thank you."

I was going to have to tell her about Jillian Crest at some point if this relationship continued. That was going to be hard.

Was I lying to her now by not divulging that very important piece of information? I looked down when her fingers tapped my knee.

"Hey, we're here."

Before I could reach for my purse, she handed the driver money, told him to keep the change, and crawled out of the cab.

"Are you coming or am I going to have to eat all of this by myself?"

I had no idea where my mind had gone during the duration of the drive. I led the way up to my place, anxious and nervous at being alone with Hope. I fluttered around my place after I opened the door, not sure what to do first. Even Clio was looking at me strangely, and he was my soul mate. I had to calm down, and only a few things helped me. I opened one of the large windows to invite the sounds in. I moved a few things around so that they wouldn't get wet, but I needed the fresh air, the calming beat of the steady rain, and the traffic below. I took a deep breath in and out.

Hope's fingers gently brushed my shoulder. "Are you okay?"

I stammered out a pained laugh. "Not really, but I'm getting there."

"Do you want me to go?" Her brow was furrowed with concern. She was very close to me. I shook my head.

"I don't want you to leave, but I don't want you to have to accommodate my quirks and anxiety attacks. And just so you know, they happen a lot." I turned to face her. "It's not fair to you."

She took my hands in hers. "Don't take this the wrong way, but just hush and let's eat. We can figure out things: you, the meaning of life, and how we are going to save the world later. Right now, I just want to share a meal, feed a cat, and sit down with a beautiful, yes, beautiful, woman. Can we do that?" She wouldn't let go of my hands until I agreed. "We don't even have to talk."

Hope took charge and directed me to sit at the couch, not the table. She found plates in the cabinet, glasses in the dishwasher, and napkins in the dispenser on the counter.

"Thank you." I took the plate and waited until she got settled on the couch, one cushion between us. "Do you want to watch anything on television?" I didn't know how to be a host. I didn't know how to entertain.

"Nope. I want to sit here in silence and eat this incredible food." She all but ignored me and started flirting with Clio. He graciously, and delicately, took a few bites of turkey from Hope's fingertips.

Traitor, I thought. It was as if I didn't exist. I ate half of my sandwich and a few chips before setting my plate to the side. I leaned back, closed my eyes, and relaxed. I hated that I couldn't be normal. Traffic had picked up because it was Saturday night, and the rain had settled into a soft pitter-patter instead of the deluge from just a few short hours ago. Even eight stories up, I could hear random voices, shouts, and bouts of laughter outside.

"Do you worry about pigeons flying in when you have the windows open?"

I turned and stared at Hope. "Well, not until just now." I jumped up and headed over to the window.

"I'm so sorry. I didn't mean to ruin it for you." Hope stood as if to help me, but didn't move.

"I can just open the windows over by the fire escape. They have screens." I wasn't upset. I was glad she brought it up. I imagined a pigeon dive-bombing me inside my own home. Clio would be a hot mess, chasing it until he either caught it or dropped dead from trying. If nothing else, he was persistent with prey. "Now can we talk?" I found that I really wanted to hear her voice.

"I thought you'd never ask." Her eyes held a playful sparkle.

I wondered how she always greeted life with a smile. She put her plate on the table beside her and repositioned herself on the couch. She slipped off her shoes, moved closer, and tucked one leg underneath her. She looked casual and completely at ease. "Are you going to be busy at work this coming week?"

"I honestly don't know. My boss told me to take a few days off, but I never know what to do with extra time, so I told him I'd just get started Monday morning like always. I'm sure the workload is piling up. I get stuck with the projects that nobody else wants for whatever reason."

"That's because you're smart and can figure things out. Just don't let them take advantage of you," she said.

People had been taking advantage of me my whole life. "I don't mind doing most of the throwaway stuff. It keeps me busy and takes my mind off things." I couldn't believe I just opened that door.

"Tell me more about yourself. I know you're a workaholic, you love math, you're a music lover, and you have a soft spot for beat-up cats." She held up four fingers and expected me to add to the list.

That made me smile. "I like to read."

"You already told me that one." She held up her thumb and had a count of five things about me. "Tell me what you like to read. Do you read science fiction? Paranormal stuff? Autobiographies? Or warm, fluffy romance books like I do?"

"I avoid romance books like the plague. I like historical books, and intrigue."

"Oh, dear God, you read algebra books for fun. I'm out

of here. Done." She made a big production of standing up and leaving.

Out of sheer instinct, I grabbed her hand. It was a big step for me and we both knew it. "Stay. Find out more about me. I owe you that much." I hesitantly released her hand and she sat down. A little closer than before. "Let's see, I like origami, jigsaw puzzles, and libraries. I spend quite a bit of time at the library. I like the crisp sound of opening a new hardback book, and the smell of age on old ones. I love museums. We are so lucky to have so many here."

"Okay, okay. Slow down. That's a lot of information to process and talk about. We need to have a date at one of the museums because I love art and you could probably teach me quite a bit. Forget about working on a jigsaw puzzle together. You see how much I struggle over music. And origami? Would you make me something sometime? Or do you have anything here? I'm always so impressed when people can concentrate so hard and make something so perfect." She seemed genuinely interested in my hobbies.

I held up my finger, indicating she was to wait just a moment, and made my way back to my office. I returned with a twisted triangle that I'd made during my very own blue period. I was proud of the blues and grays and all of the sharp angles—the way it jutted asymmetrically. I loved it because it pushed me out of my comfort zone. It was perfect in its imperfections. It made me feel normal and unsettled at once.

"I did this last winter."

She took it gently from my outstretched hands. "It's beautiful, Lily."

I watched as she gingerly moved it around in her field of vision. She was afraid of breaking it, and I appreciated her gentleness. "How long did it take you to make this?"

"I can't remember. Days at least. Some of them are really easy. I could make a small animal in about ten minutes." I shrugged like it was no big deal, but I could tell she was impressed. My pulse quickened. An urge that I hadn't felt in forever squeezed my insides and made my emotions tumble and scatter in all directions. I had to sit down. God help me, but I wanted to play for her. I wanted to sit at a piano and play something that I wrote, that I composed, just so I could have that look, that feeling she gave me again and again.

"Are you okay? You just turned white as a ghost." Hope looked at me with concern.

"I probably should eat more." I couldn't imagine eating right now, but I powered through a few more bites of my sandwich.

"Do you want to start a movie?"

"Sure, you pick." I had no idea what was good or out. Please don't pick out a romance, I thought. I watched as she scrolled through the movies.

"Oh, how about Rebecca Murphy's latest? I wanted to see it at the theaters, but we were painting the center and I was too busy to catch it. Have you seen it?"

I shook my head.

Hope's voice carried a lilt when she got excited about something. "It's a rom-com. I think you'll like it. At least, I hope you will."

"Do you need anything or want anything before we get started?" Being a hostess was stressful. She reached down and pulled out the thin, gray blanket that was rolled up in a dark wire basket under the end table. Her fingers quickly splayed the corners and fanned the threadbare keepsake of my childhood over her legs. She leaned closer to me, enough so that I could smell the hint of sandalwood on her skin and the warmth of her breath when she faced me.

"I'm ready when you are."

My eyes drifted down to her slightly parted lips when she spoke. I wanted to kiss her, but I wasn't ready to make the first move. Instead, I kicked off my shoes, tucked my legs underneath me, and hit play.

Hope snuggled into the couch as if she'd been to my place a thousand times. She automatically reached for my hand and locked her fingers with mine. The first twenty minutes were a blur. I concentrated on the gentle press of her thumb rubbing back and forth across my palm. It was hard to follow the storyline and relax when my body was on fire. Her touch won out, so I closed my eyes and enjoyed the sensation of a caress from another person. "Do you want to watch something else? Or do you want me to leave? Your eyes are closed."

"I'm not tired."

She cocked her head curiously at me. "Then why aren't you watching the movie? If this is boring, we can always turn on a documentary on the importance of algebra as an adult or the decline of dairy farms in the Midwest."

"Are you making fun of me?"

She sat up and leaned closer to me. I felt my heart kick-start when I realized she was going to kiss me. "Maybe a little bit." Her lips brushed against mine, slowly, teasingly, until I reached up and slipped my hand behind her neck to hold her close to me.

I needed a deeper connection. I wanted more. She moaned and moved closer to me, putting one hand on my leg and the other on my shoulder. I felt her hesitation, and although I appreciated her restraint, I wanted more. Twenty minutes of simple touching had me burning.

"Come here," I said. I didn't know how she could get closer without both of us stretching out next to one another on the couch, but I just knew I needed her body against mine. The forgotten movie played on as Hope slipped out from beneath my blanket and straddled my lap. I gasped and sat up straighter as our bodies touched everywhere. I wasn't nervous or scared, just unsure.

"Is this okay?" she asked, placing soft kisses on my cheeks.

"Definitely." I went with my instincts and placed one hand on her waist, and slipped the other one on the back of her neck. She moaned her appreciation. My nod encouraged her more. She deepened the kiss and held me. I finally understood chemistry between people and the desire to act on it. Every part of my body was in tune with hers. My skin tingled, my cheeks were flushed, and I was swollen in places that needed attention. I hadn't had sex with anyone before, but I knew my own body well. I needed release. When her hips pressed down and into my lap, I pushed up into her out of sheer instinct to get closer.

She broke the kiss. "Wait, wait, wait. I feel like we should slow down." Her breath was hot and fast against my lips.

"I'm okay. I promise." I cupped her face and pulled her down to me. Our passion was fierce, almost furious, and I didn't want to stop.

She pulled away again. "I know you are, but I don't know about myself," she said.

I froze and dropped my hands from her body. "I'm sorry. I didn't mean to make you feel uncomfortable."

"You didn't. At all. But I still need you to slow down."

I nodded. I hated rejection of any kind. I wasn't good with it, especially since this was the first time I'd felt something so special and open with another person. My chin started to quiver, so I looked away and focused on everything but the beautiful woman on my lap who didn't want me as much as I wanted her. The movie boomed in my ears. The rain's rhythm that pinged imperfectly only intensified my discomfort. I couldn't allow myself to cry.

Hope pulled my chin up and forced me to look at her. "Lily, I'm not uncomfortable at all. I want you. I want this. I just want to go slow. I want everything to matter. For both of us," she quickly added. She stroked my cheek until I nodded. She slipped off my lap but ensured we were still touching, still connected.

I took a deep breath. "Okay. Can we either start the movie over or try something different?"

"Let's try something else. Anything you want. Even a documentary. I could use a good nap." She smiled softly and eased back into charming Hope.

I picked a National Geographic special of a photographer and her journey through the Arctic Circle. Hope seemed genuinely interested in the subject.

"I do have one request. Can we lie on the couch? I would like for you to hold me, if that's all right?"

My smile returned. I stretched out on the couch and tucked her in front of me. I wasn't sure where to put my arm, but Hope pulled it down from the back of the couch and draped it over her waist.

"This is nice." I wasn't sure if I said it out loud, but when Hope responded I gave her a quick squeeze. A few hours before, I was a complete wreck and didn't know how this night was going to end up, but it turned out better than I expected. I knew what was in store for us and that our chemistry wasn't something to take lightly.

CHAPTER TWELVE

How do you feel about Impressionist art? Or, more importantly, what's your favorite period?" I asked. I heard Hope smile through the phone. I perked up when I heard a few notes on the piano. "Are you playing right now? Wait. Am I interrupting a lesson?"

"No, I'm just warming up. It's nice to hear from you. How are you?"

I pictured her poised at the keys, her fingertips rubbing the top of the slick ivory, itching to press down and make a sound.

"Play something for me," I said. It sounded too demanding. "I mean, I miss hearing you play. Just pretend I'm standing under the window."

"Ah, another joke from Lily Croft. I love it."

My heart catapulted in my chest at that word. Love. It wasn't one that was said to me often. I knew she was saying it without thought. People said that all the time. I just hadn't heard Hope say it before. I really liked it. I heard the phone rustle and pictured her putting it on the music rack. She played Beethoven's "Sonata in D Minor." Not only did she play the entire song, but she did it perfectly. There wasn't a single mistake. It left me breathless.

"That's a great warm-up song for me."

I didn't know what to say. I stumbled around, took a deep breath, and finally spoke. "That was brilliant, Hope. It was beautiful. Thank you for playing that for me." She was inspiring. Every aspect of her.

"Thank you. Now tell me about art. Why all the questions?" There was pride and laughter in her voice. She wanted to impress me but was embarrassed by my praise. It was sweet.

"You said you wanted me to take you to an art museum, and there's a really nice exhibit passing through that might be fun. The Art Institute is open late on Thursday. Would you like to go? Maybe we can grab dinner after?" I held my breath. If she said yes, it would be the first time I would see her since our halted makeout session. I was still embarrassed thinking about it, but when she said good night, our passion resurfaced. There was a lot of touching and kissing in my doorway until my neighbor opened his door and interrupted us on his way out for the evening.

"That sounds lovely. Do you want me to meet you at your place?"

"Why don't we just meet there at six thirty? The museum is equal distance between us and then maybe come back to my place to eat or just hang out?" Desperation clung to every word. I heard it and I'm sure she did, too.

"Even better."

"Now go play. Play music, I mean," I said.

"How's your new project?"

I smiled. She was stalling. She wanted to talk. "Meh, it's okay. I understand why everyone walked away from it."

"I don't like that your company takes advantage of you like this."

I didn't need to defend my company. I knew they were taking advantage, but they were paying me well for it.

"I'm all right with it. Really. My boss knows the crap he hands me. He knows I can go anywhere, so he compensates me well." I knew that once Gene found out about Mr. Hoyt's offer of employment, he was going to give me a bump in salary or add to my quarterly bonus.

"Okay, I'll leave it alone. For now. Get back to work. I'll see you soon."

It took me a while to get my head back into work. Hope's playing was beautiful. And she played just for me. I opened the piano app on my phone and stared at it. It was time. At least the phone screen wasn't as intimidating as it was a few weeks ago. I wiped my hands on my pants and tried to play something on the five-inch piano. I rolled my eyes at how bad it sounded and how awkward it was.

For the first time in forever, I felt brave. Maybe I was ready for the next step. I popped over to a popular shopping website and looked at all of the keyboards there. By the time I found something that would produce a decent sound, I was already in the thousands for a studio piano and a baby grand was only a few thousand more. I looked around my place. There was definitely room for it, but could I make such a commitment? What if I freaked out the minute it arrived? Baby steps. I sighed, closed out the tab, and made myself focus on work. I'd waited thirteen years to touch piano keys. I could wait a little longer.

We were in the process of securing a new client, and I needed to stay on task. I had all the numbers and statistics but couldn't focus enough to connect them into something coherent. Random losses. Deductibles. What was the probability of payout? What's the probability of Hope playing for me again? *No. Get out of my head, Hope.* I pointed to the problem on the screen to stay focused, but my mind ran away with a girl with long brown hair and red lips who kissed life back into me.

I leaned back in my chair, interlocked my fingers behind my head, and stared up at the twelve-foot-high ceiling. Was I lucky? Was Hope meant to be in my life? I felt alive for the first time in years so I knew that she was good for me, but I struggled with the thought that I just might not be good for her.

❖

"I didn't know this was fancy." Hope sipped on a glass of wine and took in our surroundings.

"Oh, stop. You look beautiful." My heart skipped when she turned to me in surprise.

"Thank you. That was sweet of you to say."

She stood in front of me wearing jeans, a sleeveless top, and strappy sandals. She fit right in. Some people were dressed in suits, but some casual patrons were in shorts and flip-flops. When in doubt, I always put on a summer dress. I was self-conscious about my pale skin in the middle of summer, but no tan lines meant I could wear anything. I was never allowed to sunbathe. It was the one thing my parents did right by me.

"Come on. Let's walk around for a bit."

My throat tightened and I pushed my heart back into place when she casually grabbed my hand and walked with me into the first room. I averted my eyes when people glanced our way.

"Does this make you uncomfortable?" She held up our joined hands.

"No. I'm just not used to it. I like it, though," I added. I loosened my grip, afraid Hope would feel the moisture that gathered on my palms. If she noticed, she was kind enough to not pull away. A walking tour with headsets was available for the exhibit, but Hope declined and asked me to tell her what I knew. My anxiety spiked. Reason number two hundred and fifty-seven of why I never wanted to be a professor.

"All right. Um. So Van Gogh found success after he died. Well, he didn't, but his work did." I felt beads of sweat push along my hairline. "Um. He was mentally ill and painted multiple versions of *Starry Night* while living in a mental institute. He died when he was pretty young after a suicide attempt that either went wrong or was successful, depending on how you look at it."

"Well, that's depressing. Do you have anything good to share about him?"

I inwardly groaned. I wasn't impressing her, I was depressing her with my knowledge. "He had good friends. His best friend was actually his brother Theo. Of course you know the story of him cutting off his own ear, right?" I asked. She nodded. "Okay, that's not really uplifting. Let's see, he painted a ton of self-portraits. You know, maybe we should grab the headset. I'm obviously really bad at this." I felt her hand squeeze mine.

"You're giving me more information than they could on one of those recordings. What else?"

Hope was genuinely interested in what I had to say, and by the end of the tour and after a glass of wine, I was far more relaxed. We both learned about the differences in American and European style and interpretation of Post-Impressionism.

"Do I know you?" A man immediately to my right startled me out of my conversation with Hope. My walls shot up and I took a step back. Hope took a step closer to position herself between me and him. "I didn't mean to interrupt your conversation, but you just look so familiar."

"No, I don't think so." I took another step back and looked for a way to anywhere else but here.

"Do you come to these events a lot? Or do you work with the museum in some capacity?" He reached out to touch me, then drew his hand back as if he suddenly remembered that was unacceptable.

If this guy whom I'd never seen before thought he knew me, he knew Jillian, not Lily. I never forgot a face. I should have known to avoid an event like this. Most music aficionados loved all art forms, especially fine arts. I still looked the same. My hair was darker than when I was younger, but it was still long, and even though I grew into my pronounced features, somebody could identify me easily enough.

"I guess she doesn't know you, sir. Please enjoy your evening. This is a great exhibit," Hope said. She gently led me away from him, her hand firmly settled on my lower back. "He was kind of rude."

I looked back at him for a flash of a second. He was studying me intently, and I desperately wanted out of there.

"Hey, are you okay? I know crowds aren't your thing. Are you ready for dinner? I'm pretty hungry."

I appreciated her efforts and nodded. "I could use something other than cheese and crackers." Community food plates always made me queasy, but I needed something in my stomach to combat my nerves and the wine. "And thank you for rescuing me. Again."

"Let's grab something on the way back to your house. I think we've seen everything here at the exhibit."

It was almost nine and I was uneasy, but I wanted alone time with Hope. She hailed a cab and we crawled in and relaxed against one another during the short ride. Hope ran her fingertips up and down my forearm—almost absently, as if she touched me every day—and talked about the night.

"I really liked the trio. As much as I love the piano, I have a deep appreciation for the violin. It looks so easy, but the manipulation of just a flick of a wrist can change the melody of something."

I smiled. I loved that she had such a deep understanding of all instruments. When I arranged my first composition, I had fits of epic proportions. I was eleven at the time, but when it was done, it was my greatest success. The violin was the hardest for me to master. I never truly conquered it.

"It's nice to hear live music again." I stiffened, knowing I'd revealed a sliver of my past without meaning to.

"You have such a good ear. Do you attend the symphony much?"

"The only music I listen to is Hope D'Marco and children who perform with her."

"Such a charmer, you are." She nudged me gently. "We should go listen to music sometime. Either classical or jazz or whatever you want. Do you listen to mainstream music?"

"You mean on the radio? No, not really." I left out the part about how I didn't have a radio in my house. Music wasn't as comforting to me as it was to her. I still felt the need to master it.

I found comfort in sounds I couldn't control—crisp steps that echoed in a long hallway, rain that impatiently drummed against my windows, birds that chirped over the heavy rustling of traffic, elevators that dinged in the distance on my floor. The only music I listened to was jazz because it was so far removed from the kind of music I composed and played. The old jazz greats like Duke Ellington and Louis Armstrong were on my phone, but I only listened in the privacy of my ear buds. There were enough sounds in everyday life to keep my mind busy.

By the time we got to my place, we were both stifling

yawns. Clio greeted us, knowing full well he was going to get bites of whatever Hope was eating. He'd given up on me. Traitor. He weaved in and out of her legs until she reached down and petted him.

"Don't worry, big boy. I have tasty cheese for you." She leaned against the counter and watched me as I got plates and drinks ready for us.

The guy at the museum who obviously recognized me from my youth really rattled me. I knew there was a very slight chance that would happen, but I had tucked that possibility into the back of my mind and filed it under the "never again" category. Just because I checked out and forgot about that life didn't mean the rest of the world forgot about me.

We ate in silence. The only noise was Clio's constant purr as he sat between us and shamelessly pawed at our plates.

I swallowed my last bite. "You've spoiled him." I was hungrier than I thought.

"He deserves it. Such a hard life out on the streets. Poor baby." She kissed the top of his head and he rubbed his jaw along her chin.

"So his dander doesn't bother you?" I'd vacuumed and cleaned right before I left to meet her tonight, but with Clio right in her face, I was sure the sneezing was going to commence any moment.

"Apparently I'm not allergic to him. Good news." Hope gave him one final bite, then gently moved him to the other side of her and scooted closer to me. "Thank you for dinner. I'm sorry our evening got ruined by some rude jerk." She ran her fingertip along my neck, and I jerked with sensitivity.

"It was still a good night. Before and now," I said.

"Such a sweet talker." She leaned over and silenced me with a soft kiss. It wasn't a passionate one, but it made me feel safe and warmed me in a different way. "I should probably go before I fall asleep right here on this couch and do something embarrassing like snore or drool."

I wanted her to stay, but I understood. I needed the downtime, too. "Can I see you this weekend?"

She played with the straps on my dress when I walked her to the door. "Basically I'm going straight to bed, I'll sleep hard, wake up, play the piano, then why don't you come over to my place? I'll cook dinner." She pulled me into her arms, her breath tickling the tiny hairs on the back of my neck as she held me close to her body. I was getting used to her nearness and I craved more.

"That sounds perfect. When do you want me?"

She lifted her eyebrow when she peeled herself off me. "Whenever you're ready."

CHAPTER THIRTEEN

C lio, I have a good feeling about this." I slipped on my light tan sandals and ran my hands over my hair in an effort to smooth down my waves.

The humidity wreaked havoc on it and there was only one thing I could do. Use product. Lots of hair product. After fifteen minutes of battling with it, I gave up and threw it back in a bun. In the winter, my hair was magical. Summertime? I couldn't pay enough for help.

"Scratch that. I had a good feeling." The frown in the mirror gave me tiny lines around my mouth that I never noticed before. I leaned in for a closer look. I wasn't even thirty yet. I frowned again, then stopped for fear of more popping up.

"What do you think? Do I pass the test?" I twisted side to side, my hands holding up my cream-colored dress. It was nice enough for a night out on the town but casual enough for a night in. I wasn't sure what Hope had in store for us, so I wanted to be prepared. I grabbed my purse and headed for the train station. I planned to arrive before they were done at the Center so maybe I'd hear Hope play. She had left it up to me to decide what time we got together tonight. I planned on following her home like a stray. Last night ended in a fizzle, and tonight I wanted sparks. Maybe fireworks.

"Do you want to come in, Lily?" Agnes approached the stairs where I was sitting.

"I was waiting to hear Hope play. It's kind of our thing." I was embarrassed at getting caught, but not enough to move.

"Well, you might be waiting a while. I think this afternoon is nothing but paperwork. Grants are due." She looked like she wanted to say more, but buttoned up once I showed interest. "Why don't you come and wait inside. You look a little flushed." It didn't help that it was almost five in the afternoon in the dead of summer. The sun feathered its way between the tall buildings and landed on the stoop beside me.

"Thank you. That's not a bad idea." I stood and followed Agnes inside.

"You can either wait down here or head up to her office. I'm sure she would like to see you, though." Agnes winked at me and headed into the first therapy room.

I was torn between racing up the steps to see Hope right away, and relaxing on the couch as if I hadn't given her much thought other than to casually stop in and say hello, more of an afterthought. I sat on the cool leather for about thirty seconds. I crossed my legs, then uncrossed them. Reached for a magazine, then dropped it three inches from where I picked it up. I heard Agnes strike a few keys on the piano. The sound was distantly quiet, slipping out from beneath the tiny slit between the door and the carpet. It enveloped me in the silence of the foyer. Most Friday afternoons were chaotic in the city. I picked over the sounds like fruit at a neighborhood stand. Only the best, and only what satisfied me. Today I listened to Agnes for twenty seconds before making my decision and heading for the stairs.

"Come in."

I smiled as though I had a secret as I turned the knob to Hope's office. The smile she gave me when she looked up from her paperwork took my breath away. It lit up my heart and gave me a surge of energy. I clutched the handle and waved the door open a few inches back and forth until I saw Hope look down at my hand.

"Or you can stand there and fan me. The breeze feels good."

"I'm sorry." I left the door open, then turned around to shut it. I couldn't be more awkward right now if I tried. Downstairs, I was the epitome of cool, at least in my head.

Hope stood up and walked around her desk to greet me. She wore tan slacks and a sleeveless black blouse that showed off her toned arms. Her hair was pinned up and she wore a little bit more makeup than I was used to seeing on her. She looked professional, and hot as hell. She brushed her lips over mine in an innocently erotic way and whispered hello. The kiss lasted about two seconds, but the aftershocks were paralyzing. I couldn't move.

"Come have a seat. Tell me about your day and why you're surprising me here at work."

"Time. I thought since we were both tired last night, we could take advantage of more time today." I stopped my twisting hands and relaxed them in my lap.

She leaned up against her desk and crossed one ankle over the other. I swallowed hard as my eyes traveled down to her three-inch heels and back up to meet her eyes. She smirked. I resisted leaning back in my chair at her nearness, not because I was uncomfortable but because I wanted to reach out and touch her. I wanted to bury my face against her thighs and open myself up to her in a way I hadn't before. The thought was extreme.

"Tell me about your day." She played with the little charm on her gold necklace, moving it back and forth, slowly.

"Not much to tell. Crunched a few numbers, sent a few

emails. It looks as though you had quite the day. You look amazing."

"I had a few money meetings today. They are never fun, but necessary." She blew out a heavy sigh.

I watched as one sexy tendril of hair fell against the side of her cheek, just brushing her ear. "I'm sure they were successful."

Her smile was small and wavered. She shrugged and moved around to the other side of the desk. I missed her nearness. "I won't know for a while. A lot of *maybe* and *perhaps*. I try to hit up local businesses, but a lot of them already have charities and can only donate so much."

So much flashed through my mind at once. B&T, Banks Corporation, myself. I felt a fierceness rise inside me. I tamped it down quickly. I couldn't help. Nobody knew me, and it wasn't my problem. I didn't want to get involved, but I didn't want Hope to fail.

"Hey, no worries. We'll get it worked out. We always do. Now, let me just send out a quick email and I'm all yours," she said.

I watched as she quickly composed a message. She was so focused as her fingers flew across the keyboard. I smiled when she played with her bottom lip, pinching the sides together to form a "U" as she reread what she just wrote.

She winked at me, hit the Send button dramatically, locked her computer, and grabbed her purse from the bottom drawer of her desk. "Let's start our night early, shall we?" She playfully pounced on me, trapping me in the chair.

I leaned up and pulled her down to me. Her mouth curled into a smile right before my lips captured hers. I thought it was going to be a quick kiss. I had no intention of staying longer than we needed to, but she pulled me to my feet and I pushed into her. When the back of her legs hit the desk, she scooted back to sit on the top, scattering pens and highlighters and other things I didn't care about. I ran my hands up her arms, over her neck, and held her face while I kissed it. I pulled out the pins that held her beautiful hair and dug my fingertips into the waves as they cascaded down her back.

She moaned and pressed into me. Her hands moved to my waist, my hips, my ass. I gasped when she gave it a little squeeze. "Is this okay?" she asked against my mouth.

I nodded and captured her mouth in another kiss. I sucked her bottom lip and scraped my teeth over it. That was apparently the right thing to do. She grabbed the back of my head and slipped her tongue deep inside my mouth. Gone was the gentle Hope who held back. I was consumed by her. When I realized my hands were on her thighs, spreading her apart so I could get closer to her, I stopped. We were both panting and just short of tearing off one another's clothes.

"So maybe we should get out of here." Her voice was shaky, and I couldn't help but feel smug. Me and my zero experience had this gorgeous woman panting. I was doing something right. I knew my body was on fire, but it was nice to know hers was, too.

"Definitely." I stood and straightened my dress. I wasn't too wrinkled, not that it mattered. I just needed to keep my hands busy. We were standing very close and I was still slightly off after we separated.

"Hey." Hope's voice was low and sexy.

I looked up from patting my imaginary wrinkles.

"Thank you for coming to pick me up. It was a sweet and very delicious idea." I subconsciously licked my bottom lip, surprised at the taste of her still on my mouth. Peppermint and warmth.

"And stop looking sexy because we'll never leave here." She opened the door and gave me a gentle push out into the hall. "What is it about you in my office that makes me lose control like that?"

❖

It was my first time at Hope's place. Her apartment was small, but she made the most of the space.

"I love it," I said, and really meant it. It was her. Bright, modest, and comforting. I sat on the plush couch and ran my hands over the texture. The soft ridges tickled my palms.

"Don't get too comfortable. You're going to help me in there." She pointed behind me.

I feigned shock and put my hand over my heart. "What? You aren't going to cook for me?"

"Lily Croft's humor is starting to show again." She winked at me and crooked her finger for me to follow her.

I sighed, dramatically rolled my eyes, and made a big production out of getting off the couch.

"We are going to cook for us." She pulled an apron covered in musical notes off a hook in the pantry and handed it to me.

I smiled, slipped it over my head, and tied it in a bow behind me.

Hope reached up and fixed a twist in the material at my neck. Her fingers lingered against the side of my neck, caressing up and down.

My eyes fluttered shut and I tilted my head to give her easier access. When her touch dropped to my collarbone, I shivered and opened my eyes again. Her brown eyes were sharp. The way she looked at me made me shiver a second time.

"I thought we were going to cook, not that I'm complaining," I said.

"You're right. Might as well take advantage of you while

you're so agreeable." She winked at me and turned to get things started.

My blush went unnoticed. She confused me in such a charmingly frustrating way. One minute she told me we need to slow down, the next she ignited me with a single touch or fiery kiss. For the first time ever, I understood raw passion. The need to touch her and continue to touch her flourished inside me. She had woven her way into my daily thoughts. No, hourly. It was hard not to think about her.

"What are we having?" I peeked over her shoulder, accidentally bumping her from behind. She moaned and covered it up with a small cough. I was mortified, yet a sliver of sexual power rose up in my chest. She wanted me. She stood up straight and I stepped back.

"I was thinking grilled chicken breasts and steamed vegetables. I can make some pasta if you'd like. It's been so hot out that I haven't had much of an appetite."

"I'm good with ice cream for dinner."

Hope laughed. "That doesn't make me a great hostess. I want to cook for you. We can have ice cream for dessert. In the meantime, will you slice the vegetables?" She stacked broccoli, mushrooms, three different peppers, and asparagus on the counter and pointed to a wood block that housed all the knives I needed.

I grabbed one and started dicing each vegetable with precision and just the right amount of thickness.

"These look perfect. And you told me you don't like to cook."

"I don't like to only because it's hard to cook for just myself. I end up with a lot of leftovers that I forget about. Since I don't really like people and I hate being out in crowds, I learned to cook a long time ago."

"I always help my mom with Sunday dinner. It's relaxing

and a chance for us to bond. My brothers are a handful, but very sweet. I think you'll like them." She assumed that I would meet her family. I wasn't so sure. I had a feeling Hope came from a rambunctious family. She'd already warned me they were loud. I couldn't imagine trying to adapt to that many stimuli. "So did you ever take cooking classes?"

"My culinary skills are compliments of the internet. It's incredible what you can learn on YouTube."

"I don't have the patience to watch something unless it's in person," she said.

"We are so opposite."

"Opposites attract." She winked at me again and grabbed dishes to plate our food.

We sat at her kitchen nook to eat, side by side. It was nice being close instead of five feet apart with a table between us. She touched me from time to time on my arm or my leg when she got animated telling a story. My body brimmed with energy. I knew tonight was going to be special. I was relaxed and alone with a beautiful woman. I helped her clean up even though she insisted I not lift a finger. She poured us each a glass of Roscato and excused herself.

"I'm going to leave you for ten minutes. I need to freshen up and slip into something more comfortable like a T-shirt and shorts. Make yourself at home." She playfully pecked my cheek and disappeared down the hall.

I bravely walked around her apartment and looked at her framed family photos scattered throughout. Hope's family was gorgeous, which was no surprise to me. I touched books she presumably read and thumbed through sheets of music stacked on her bookshelf. Classical music and contemporary mainstream, which surprised me at first but made sense when I remembered she worked with kids who were probably into contemporary music. I brushed my fingertips over a Selmer case that rested against the bookshelf. Curiosity won out and I opened it. Much to my delight, I found a beautiful saxophone. I didn't touch it because it was rude to touch somebody's instruments without their permission, especially ones that cost thousands of dollars. On the other side of the bookshelf, I found a Buffet Crampon clarinet, also housed in a crushed velvet-lined case. I didn't see a piano, but I knew that somebody who played as well as she did had an outlet. I guessed she had a keyboard somewhere either under the couch, in a closet, or maybe even a small studio piano in her office or bedroom. The quick tour she gave me earlier included her pointing to closed doors and telling me "there's the office" and "that's my bedroom."

I was in her kitchen when she returned and felt guilty for no other reason than I wasn't still on the couch. I was excited at my finds in her apartment. Genuine happiness filled my heart.

CHAPTER FOURTEEN

You look guilty about something, but your smile is throwing me off."

Busted and I didn't even care. "I confess. I saw something by the bookcase I liked."

She walked over to me, her small hips barely holding up a pair of shorts that I doubt she wore out in public. And her double layered white-over-red tank tops left very little to the imagination. She wasn't wearing a bra, and I was trying my damnedest not to stare.

"Only something by the bookcase? Not more?" She linked her fingers with mine. "Maybe something right in front of you?"

"Definitely something that's right in front of me." It felt natural to kiss her. I leaned over and pulled her toward me until we both moaned slightly. What started out as a playful kiss turned passionate quickly. Her tongue stroked mine, and within seconds, we were both moaning.

"Mmm. I think I really like this side of you." She crossed her hands behind my neck and played with my hair. I tried hard not to close my eyes, but I couldn't help it. I liked her touch. "So what else did you find that you liked?"

I opened my eyes and nodded in the direction of the

bookcase. "I saw a beautiful saxophone over there. I know I shouldn't have opened the case, but I was curious what was in it."

"I spent a lot of money on it, and it was so worth it." She pulled me to the couch so we could relax. She smelled clean and her hair was wet from the shower.

"Will you play it for me? I don't mean right now, just some time in the very near future."

"I probably should practice more than I do, but yes, I would love to." She blushed with self-consciousness.

"Come on. You're fine playing the piano in front of me." I reached for her hand because I wanted her warmth. She scooted closer to me.

"The piano is my true love. I don't get very many opportunities to play the saxophone because only a few kids at the center want to learn it. Everyone wants to study the guitar or violin. Don't get me wrong. Both are great instruments, but the saxophone is so sexy," she said.

She had a point. It was sensuous both in the way your body moved when you played it, and the sounds it produced.

"Where's your piano or keyboard? You have to have one around here somewhere."

"I have a keyboard in the office. A piano would be wonderful, but my neighbors would hate me."

Hope brought up another good point. I rarely saw my neighbors. I wanted to keep it that way.

"Thankfully, I can play during the day whenever I want," she said.

"I miss hearing you play."

"I miss you stalking me."

I feigned innocence. "I don't know what you're talking about. One day I walked by this building and some woman leaned out and started yelling at me. It was just so weird." The lilt of her laugh made me smile. I was capable of entertaining someone. Someone I liked.

"I love this playful side of you."

My heart skipped when she said "love." I sat up a little straighter. "It's nice to be with someone who gets me so thank you for being you."

She leaned forward and kissed me. It was a swift kiss. "Should we try a movie? Maybe this time we should do a comedy and I'll sit over here on my side of the couch, and you sit on your side."

I responded by pulling her closer to me. I was still very much aware of her lack of clothing, and my body tingled in all the right places. My peripheral vision was stellar.

"I want you close to me. I missed you today."

She looked at my mouth. "I missed you, too. Last night was nice, because I like being seen with you, but I like the intimacy of just us at my place or at yours."

Our lips had found the perfect rhythm when we kissed. Her warm, wet mouth took control and I moaned as her tongue touched mine. I wanted more, though. I needed more. I pulled her down with me. She slipped into the tight space between me and the back of the couch and broke our kiss only to get comfortable. She rested one of her legs over mine and gauged my reaction before moving forward. I reached down and touched her bare thigh. I already loved her shorts. My fingers shook slightly as I caressed her smooth thigh.

She leaned up a bit and watched me touch her. "Is this okay?"

I nodded but didn't speak. I was close to being over-whelmed, but in a good way. The kind where you quickly build up energy and have to expel it or else explode. I traced the tiny freckles on her legs while she placed small, delicate kisses on my neck and cheek. It was driving me crazy. She was driving me crazy. I was afraid to try anything beyond this for fear that she would reject the idea of taking it to the next level. I expanded my range of touch and slipped just my fingertip under the hem of her shorts. Her breath hitched next to my ear, and for a second, I thought I did something wrong.

"Is this okay?" It was my turn to ask the question and her turn to nod. My confidence was off the chart at the moment. My caresses grew bolder. The unguarded look she gave me was pure with a hint of vulnerability. I stared into her eyes and tried to convey that I was okay with this. That I was ready for us to try new things. Hope was waiting for me to make the first move.

I scooted up and faced her so that we mirrored one another. She touched me wherever I touched her. It wasn't a game, really, but more a consensual willingness to explore one another. I leaned on my elbow and ran my fingertips up her side, her arm, and back down. Chill bumps popped up on her arms and legs. When her nipples hardened, I couldn't help but want to touch her breasts. I touched her stomach and moved my hand slowly, carefully up to her breast. Hope moaned when my palm grazed the hard pebble and impatiently wrapped her hand over mine and pressed it to her body.

She was so soft, so full, so responsive to my touch. She arched her back so her body was closer to mine and captured my lips in another possessive kiss. I cupped her breast, massaged for a few seconds, then closed my fingers around her rock-hard nipple. I wanted that softness and hardness in my mouth. I broke our kiss and slid the thin tank tops straps down so they rested on her arm. I kissed the top of her cleavage and gently pulled the double layer down until I freed her breast. Her hand found its way to the back of my head and guided my mouth down. We both wanted the same thing. She let me be gentle at first. I sucked the soft roughness of her areola and her nipple into my mouth and swirled my tongue in circles over it. Her loud moans and writhing body were encouraging. I felt her hips push against me the harder I sucked. She pushed me up and, for a split second, I thought she was rejecting me again.

"Did I do something wrong?" My heart picked up speed as I thought I'd hurt her, or embarrassed her, or even made her feel uncomfortable.

She touched my face in a soothing gesture. "Not at all."

She sat up briefly and removed both tanks. I stared at an almost naked Hope. She reached to pull me back to her, but stopped and dropped her hands to her sides. She wanted me to see her, to take my own time. I was in awe. She had such a tiny waist and full breasts. I rested my palm on her flat stomach and caressed up to the underside of her breasts and back down to the top of her shorts. I bravely dipped my fingertips in the waistband and ran them back and forth from hip to hip. She hooked her leg over the back of the couch. I didn't know where to start, but I knew Hope had given me permission to do whatever I wanted. She was ready.

"I have touched a lot of beautiful things in my life, but you, Hope D'Marco, are by far the loveliest." I spoke from the heart.

Caressing her was better than any instrument I'd played, held, and mastered. I was fascinated with the smoothness of her body and the way her breath caught when I reached a sensitive spot. My hands caressed her skin. I was making music out of her sharp intakes of breath and soft moans. I stroked the soft skin on the inside of her thigh. She lifted her hips the closer my hand got to her core. I wasn't ready for that, so I skimmed up her shorts and placed my hand comfortably on her stomach. She was holding back for my sake. I leaned over her and kissed her.

She reached for me and moved my hips so I was resting

completely between her legs. It was erotic being dressed while Hope only had a tiny pair of shorts on. Her legs wrapped around my waist for just a moment and our cores touched. I gasped. She slid her legs back down so they were still entwined with mine, but we weren't as connected.

"I'm sorry about that." She paused, her voice barely audible and very raspy. It sounded so sexy. "You make me forget about things."

"Don't be sorry. I love all of this. I'm serious when I say you are beautiful." I kissed her swollen lips.

My body was blossoming with the need to release, but it was so amazing to share this with another person, I didn't know what to do. I wanted to stay on this plateau of sexual excitement where everything was sensitive and new, but I had this desire to please Hope. I knew what I liked on my body, but I didn't want to assume she enjoyed the same things. I moved back down to her breasts, giving both equal attention. Her body was flushed with desire. I kissed her again and again until I got lost in our motions. Then I forgot about everything except pleasing her. I couldn't help but rock my hips into her as much as she couldn't help pushing back into me. My dress had ridden up somewhere between my knees and thighs so when our skin touched, I almost lost control. She was so warm and silky against me. Hope dug her fingers into my back and slid down until she cupped my ass. A new sensation and one I thoroughly enjoyed.

"Just like that, Lily. Just like that." She breathed her words into my mouth. I had no idea what she meant, but I didn't stop moving or kissing her until I felt her body tighten and stiffen under mine and she broke our kiss to cry out. Never in my life had I experienced something so raw and powerful. Her entire body shook, and the only thing I could think to do was hold her. She clutched me until her body settled against mine.

"That." She paused and continued after catching her breath. "That wasn't supposed to happen. I'm so embarrassed." She covered her face with her hands.

"Are you kidding me? This is the best night of my life." Pride made me want to jump up and dance, sing, yell with happiness, but the look on Hope's face kept me grounded. "Hope, look at me. You did absolutely nothing wrong."

"But I made this big production the other night about waiting until we were both ready," she said.

"We are both ready." I kissed her softly.

She gave me a quick, tight squeeze and nodded.

I jumped guiltily when we heard loud knocking.

"Why aren't you answering your phone? I know you're home." The voice on the other side of the door was deep and demanding and scared the shit out of me.

I watched as Hope yanked on her tank tops and adjusted her shorts. "Fuck."

"Who is that?" I was in full panic mode. I went from gentle, tender first-time lover to paranoid freak in the span of two seconds. The banging didn't stop. I started pacing.

"Calm down, Bobby. I'll be there in a second," Hope called.

Who the hell was Bobby? My panic turned into jealousy. Who was this guy and why was he here? Hope walked to the door, unlocked it, and opened the door to a very tall, very muscular man who grabbed her and swung her around right in front of me. My hands balled into fists as I watched their exchange.

"Well, well, well, little sister. Pardon the interruption, but you should've answered the phone. We're in town this weekend and I wanted to surprise you. Who is this beauty?" He reached out to me and I shrank back in fear. My mind processed that this was her brother, but why was he here? And why right now? I glanced at the clock. It was early, only eight.

"Bobby, this is my girlfriend, Lily. Lily, this is my older, obnoxious brother Bobby, who lives in New York and I miss him, but whose timing stinks."

Hope pulled on a T-shirt she had conjured out of thin air or from some hidden place I missed. It wasn't as if I was concentrating on her. My attention was solely on her brother. I was the worst judge of human behavior, but even I knew their vibe was off. Wait a minute. Did she just introduce me as her girlfriend? I turned to her.

"You look familiar," Bobby said to me, then turned to Hope. "Has she been to one of our dinners before?"

"No, Bobby. You've never met her," Hope said. She was irritated, hopefully at his intrusion only.

That was my cue. I couldn't be there any longer. "Hope, I'm going to go now. I'll just see you tomorrow, okay?"

She looked at me as though she couldn't believe I would leave right then. I leaned toward her so only she could hear. "He's here to stay. I'm perfectly okay. Call me later?" I placed a small, gentle kiss on her cheek.

She wasn't happy about any of this—well, maybe what happened between us, but not about her brother showing up. I didn't want her to have to decide. This brother was from out of town. I lived in the same city.

"It was nice meeting you, Bobby."

He smiled and muttered something responsive, and I bolted. My dress was a wrinkled mess, my hair had unraveled into something unmanageable. I practically jogged to the station. Friday evening, albeit early, was still iffy for me on the train. Not because I didn't feel safe, but because a different crowd took it on the weekends and nights out. I opted for a cab because I just couldn't deal with any more stimuli. I needed time to process everything that had happened before Bobby banged on the door. I gave the cabbie my address, buckled in, and closed my eyes. Tonight was incredible. So many things happened, but the most exciting thing was that I had a girlfriend. One I was proud of and deliriously happy to have in my life. She was so sweet, and gentle, and made me feel like I was the only person in the world who mattered to her. I was half of something perfect. The other half, my half, still needed serious work, but I was trying even though that meant stepping out of my comfort zone. The reward was totally worth it.

Chapter Fifteen

I'm so sorry my brother showed up." The strain in Hope's voice was clear.

It was eight in the morning, and even though my sleep had been punctuated by me waking up every half hour to check my phone, I was up and ready for the day.

"It's okay. Really. I know your family is important to you, and I know Bobby doesn't get in town as much as you would like." I nodded at my answer as if I was trying to convince both of us. My eyes burned from lack of sleep. I rubbed them and pressed my cool fingertips to my eyelids, providing a few seconds of relief.

"He didn't leave until late. We had a few things to discuss." She stumbled over her words. Before I could ask the details, my manners kicked in. Hope would tell me if she wanted me to know. I trusted her.

"Are you okay?"

"Yeah, I just hate that our night got ruined. I'm sorry about that," she said.

"Last night was great. It didn't get ruined. I told you, it was the best night of my life." It really was. Better than any concert I'd seen or performed.

"Do you want to get together for breakfast this morning, or do you have plans?"

I almost snorted. She was the only person I hung out with. "Yes. There's a little breakfast shop a few blocks from here that I want to try. Can you come this way?" I'd wanted to try it now that I was back to working from home, but I was thinking of placing an order to go. But I'd much rather have a sit-down meal with my girlfriend. I smiled. Of course a Saturday morning meant a two-hour wait. I went online and made reservations for nine thirty while Hope tried to figure out what time she could be ready by. "If you want to meet me there at nine thirty, we should have a table ready."

"That sounds great. I will see you soon."

We hung up and I raced to my closet. I decided on navy capris, a white sleeveless top, and sandals. Very neutral, very plain. I was going to have to rethink my wardrobe. I wanted to look good for Hope, not be boring, but almost everything in my closet was earth toned. I had very little color. I felt bland. I'd worn all of my nicer casual clothes around her, and my wardrobe was beginning to cycle. I needed to go shopping.

Of course I got to the restaurant early, but I checked in and waited outside for Hope. It was a nice, sunny day and I was too excited to sit. The place was packed, but I didn't feel too out of place, yet.

"Do not burn that beautiful skin." Hope slid her arm around my waist and kissed me in front of all of Chicago, and I didn't mind. For the first time, I wasn't worried about what people thought or if they were looking at me.

"Good morning." I had the cheesiest grin on my face and I didn't care.

"It is now," she said and kissed me again.

I leaned into her. Just a few short hours ago, I had this woman almost naked in my arms. "Are you hungry?"

Her eyes narrowed sexily at me. She tilted her chin up a bit and raised an eyebrow. "Definitely."

I smiled. "Great. Let's go inside." I looked at my app. "We're next."

She touched my arm to get my attention. "Are you going to be okay inside?"

"I'm feeling pretty good this morning." Even though I didn't sleep the greatest, I was on cloud nine. When we walked in, we were seated almost immediately at the back of the restaurant. I sat in the chair with my back against the wall. "So, your brother came by."

She laughed. "At the worst possible time." She reached out and squeezed my hand. Unspoken words passed between us.

"Is everything okay?"

She shrugged and sighed. "No. Not really."

"Do you want to talk about it?"

"Leading Note is losing money from the company my brother works for. Every year they pick a charity or organization to help, and we've been the recipient for the last two years. I knew we were going to lose their funding since the company relocated to New York, but I was hoping for another year during their transition. It's just a hard hit." She stirred her coffee until the sound drove me crazy and I had to reach out and touch her hand.

"There are so many companies where you are now that would surely give Leading Note funding." My mind went into overdrive. I thought of Banks Corporation, B&T, and knew they were rolling in the dough. They most likely had money set aside for charity. It was all about tax breaks with most corporations. "Are you the one who reaches out to companies?"

"Yes, but I don't know that I love this location. In all fairness, Bobby's company leases the building. That's how we were able to get it for a steal this year, but since they moved and their lease ends, if the owner allows us to stay, the price will probably triple next year. I would much rather find something where we were before. We lost a lot of kids when we were forced out."

"What happened to your last place?"

"The building sold and the new owner converted it into condos."

"That's crazy." I was shocked. There was so much money in the city and why more companies couldn't—no, wouldn't give more was beyond me.

"Yeah, so we've been limping along this year. If I can't come up with more money, we'll probably have to either close or move to the suburbs where the whole idea of the center is wasted." She was crushed.

"I'm so sorry." I had walked away from my life and everything I worked hard for because they weren't my dreams, but to love something that much and have it taken away because of funding was disheartening.

"Enough about that." She waved her hand like her life wasn't in turmoil and her dreams weren't about to go up in smoke. "Tonight there is this little jam session at a club that isn't technically open to the public until next weekend. It just popped up. I'd like to take you. It's very informal and will only be a handful of people. It's jazz, and I know how much you enjoy it. Will you go with me?"

I waited two seconds, picked up my coffee cup with both hands, and said yes over the rim. The way her face lit up, especially after the hardships she just shared with me, showed how good her heart was. I would be wallowing in self-pity if faced with half of Hope's problems.

"It sounds fun." And it really did. I was at a point where I thought I could handle it. I pictured a small round table in the back of the room where we sat shoulder to shoulder and could touch one another discreetly. A candle rested on the table and cast shadows of our silhouettes on the wall behind us. I romanticized it, a new trait I was discovering about myself.

"And whenever you want, we can leave. I'm not under any obligation to be there."

"You probably know a lot of musicians in town, huh?" I wasn't jealous, just curious. I had a list of instrumentalists and conductors in my head that I liked but never contacted. My meltdown was very public and very embarrassing. Once I decided to pick myself up, I was an adult and wanted nothing to do with that life. Now I was starting to rethink things. Music was always going to be a part of me whether I wanted it to or not.

"Some locals like what we are doing and want to help out. Plus, I love live music, all kinds, and whenever there's an opportunity to play, I do. You can meet all kinds of people, and some of them are really into what the center is about."

"Wait. Are you going to play?" I was shocked. I knew what a jam session was, but I just thought we'd be in the audience.

She shrugged at me. "Maybe. Just depends on how many people show up." Hope had no fear. She was my polar opposite. I was breaking out in a sweat for her, and we weren't even at the venue. "I think it will be fun." Her eyes were on me, gauging my reaction. I tried to keep my anxiety from showing, but tapping my spoon on the table was a dead giveaway that I was worried. "And I think it will be good for you to be around this kind of music." She reached out and held my hands. "We'll be okay. I'll be right there with you."

Hope was a genuinely good person without a selfish bone in her body. Her will and determination was inspiring. I fell in love with her in that moment. The waitress topped off our coffees and told us our food would be out in a few minutes. I stood. Hope did, too.

"Are you okay?" Hope asked.

I stared at her as the realization of the moment seeped into my bones. It was both frightening and exhilarating. My heartbeat drummed in all of my body parts. I throbbed with fear and an unidentifiable emotion that finally showed itself as love. Worst timing ever.

"Um, yeah, yes. I'm fine." I sank slowly in my chair and avoided stares from the people around us.

"Do we need to go?"

"No. No, I'm fine. I'm sorry about that." Weirdo me showed up at the worst possible times. I reached for my tiny glass of water and downed it fast. The food arrived, but I wasn't hungry. I could barely look Hope in the eye.

"Let's just go."

I reached out and touched her hand. "I'm sorry. I'm fine. Really. Let's have a good meal." I pleaded with her until she believed me. Picking at my omelet and the giant biscuit on my plate under the guise of eating, I encouraged her to continue our conversation. It took effort for me to swallow. All of my senses were on overdrive and my throat was constricted with the heaviness of my sudden realization. Sounds were louder, smells were stronger, and heat blossomed in my chest and swelled against my ribs. Love was strange and not at all like I was led to believe in movies and books.

"Lily?"

I snapped out of my daydream. "What?"

"Are you ready to go?" Hope had already paid the bill and I completely missed it.

"Sure. I'm sorry. I don't know where I just went." I followed her out of the restaurant and blinked in the bright sun. It was getting hotter earlier in the day.

Hope slipped on a pair of sunglasses and reached for my hand. "What are you doing right now?"

I wanted time to myself to process last night and this morning. I needed to get away from her, but I didn't want to leave her side. I was in a quandary. My thoughts scattered like pick-up sticks and I grasped for anything solid. "I have a few things to do before tonight. Do you mind if we just meet up later today?"

She pulled me into her arms. My stomach quaked like a trapped animal. I was afraid she could feel my trembling, but she carried on as if holding me was something we did every day.

"I get it. Can you come over to my house at eight? Since the club is closer to my place."

"I'll be there." I kissed her again and walked in the opposite direction to be alone with my thoughts. I was in love and yet I was running away from it. I called Dr. Monroe but got her answering service. I was going to have to deal with this breakthrough on my own. I tuned out the world and all of its noises and concentrated on my feelings even though I already knew what they meant.

CHAPTER SIXTEEN

You look incredible." Hope opened the door, gave me a look over, and pulled me into her arms for a passionate kiss. Just the sight of her kicked my heart rate up a few notches and made me hold her a little tighter.

"So do you." I pulled back to get a better view of her tight outfit. She was wearing black pants and a black pullover that showed off her curves. I tingled just remembering those curves pressing against my body last night. I was ready to pick up from where we left off, but I had a feeling I was going to have to wait.

"We have a few minutes if you want to sit down for a bit." She tried to sound nonchalant, but her voice was huskier and her skin was warm and flushed.

My girlfriend wanted a quick makeout session. Images of last night flashed continuously in my mind as I pulled her to the couch and sat down. She surprised me by straddling my lap. I ran my hands up and down her thighs.

"We don't even have to go if you don't want to," I said. I smiled because that was something she would have said to me.

"I want to go, but I'd like a little private time with you first."

I didn't have time to respond. Her mouth pressed against mine, hungrily, greedily. My hands slid up to her waist and I pulled her closer against me. I softly pressed into her, eliciting a delicious moan that started deep in her chest and landed against my lips. We spent a solid ten minutes grinding against one another until I stopped us and carefully removed my hands from underneath her shirt.

"If we don't leave now, we're staying here." I tried to lighten the mood. "Plus, I think I'm wrinkling you." I already knew I was a mess.

She pressed her forehead against mine and sighed. We were both breathing hard. My body was swollen and throbbing in all of the sensitive places I wanted her to touch. I felt her nod.

"You're right. We can pick this back up later."

She slowly untangled herself from my body. I almost whimpered with regret. I slid my hand into hers and she pulled me up. She looked at my lips and licked hers. We were so close, physically and emotionally, but now was not the time. Hope had to be somewhere and I needed to respect that. I wanted to smile and shake this feeling, but this feeling was love, and I had fallen too hard and too deep to brush it off. I was at a loss for words.

"The bar is just a few blocks down. Are you sure you're up for this? I can cancel," she said.

"Let's go. I'll be fine." I almost believed myself. If it got overwhelming, I would just slip out for a minute or concentrate on Hope.

I was pleasantly surprised when she reached for her saxophone.

"You're going to play tonight? Then we are definitely going."

"You mean there was a chance we would stay here and not go?" She tried to joke about it, but we both felt the heaviness of the moment.

I pulled her to me. "Somebody once said we had all the time in the world and we shouldn't rush things."

She hung her head. "Yeah, and look at what happened. I pounced on you last night."

I cupped her chin and lifted it so that she would look into my eyes. "You didn't do anything that I didn't want, too. We've discussed this. We're both adults, and last night was so incredibly special and important to me. Don't worry so much."

"You are entirely too perfect, Lily Croft," she said.

I snorted. "You know me better than that. I'm a hot mess on most days. Thank you for keeping me grounded."

❖

"Wow." That's the only thing I could think of when we walked into the place. Hope's friend Miles unlocked the door and quickly ushered us in. There were about thirty people in the room and eight onstage. I felt myself internally shrink at all of the activity. So many people were talking, laughing, drinking, and then there was the music onstage. My mind tried to shut out everything and concentrate, but we were passed from couple to couple as Hope tried to work her way to the stage. She grabbed my hand and held me close to her body as she answered questions and hugged everybody who recognized her. Hope D'Marco was very popular in this scene. I was oddly proud of her as I watched her talk with her friends. She was quick to introduce me to them and faster to lead me away.

"Do you want to sit at a table by yourself or onstage off to the side? Which would be more comfortable for you?"

I pointed to a booth that was off to the side. "That looks good. I can still see you and the rest of the musicians."

She made sure I was comfortable before she left to order us drinks. I took a few deep breaths and focused on the rhythm of music onstage. There was laughter and a quick discussion about notes, but the musicians fell into a rhythm that I felt deep in my bones. I smiled. The music didn't make me anxious.

"Here you go." Hope set a glass in front of me. "A mojito will hit you in all the right spots."

The rum immediately assaulted my senses when I leaned in to get a whiff of the ingredients. This was a strong drink, but it also had a hint of sweetness. I smacked my lips in approval after the first sip. This was delicious and was going to get me into trouble. I'd have to go slow.

"Hey, I'm fine. Go play. I want to hear you." I swear she blushed. I found it endearing that she was nervous to play in front of me.

She unlatched the case and gently lifted the saxophone out and secured it around her neck. She kissed me softly, popped the reed in her mouth to moisten it, and made her way to the stage. I was amazed at how quickly she fell into the pickup song after only listening to a few notes. She was fantastic. The best one up there. She had complete control, and I knew every single note she played was for me. I wanted to close my eyes and just listen and absorb the music, but I couldn't take my eyes off Hope. She was confident and sure even though just last night she told me she needed to practice more.

Last night. I leaned back in the booth and thought about last night. The smile on my face couldn't have been larger. I absently twirled the empty mojito glass in front of me and thought about how different my life was twenty-four short hours ago. I never expected my feelings to be so powerful or that I would be so sure of something. I wanted to touch her. I wanted her to touch me, but she let me move at my own pace.

After playing for about half an hour, Hope bowed out and headed toward me with two glasses of water.

"You were incredible," I said.

She beamed at me, her smile warming me from the inside. "I'm glad I slipped right in. I was afraid I would stumble around up there, but it was fun." She drank half of her water before she sat across from me in the booth. The music was still loud, but we were far enough away to have a conversation.

"Are you done or just taking a break?" I was surprised that my anxiety was at an all time low.

"I think I'm done. It's hard for two saxophones to compete and I just wanted to hang out here for a minute or two."

"I'm having a good time. Thank you for including me."

She held my hand across the table. "I'm happy you decided to come. I know how much you appreciate music and how hard it is for you to be in a crowd."

"Well, hiding out in this booth isn't really being submerged in a crowd. Nobody even knows I'm here." My anxiety was under control and I was able to enjoy the music onstage even though Hope wasn't up there. Flushed from playing, with a smile from ear to ear, she was very adorable.

"Scoot over. I want to sit next to you." She stood up and sat next to me on the bench.

Her body was warm and there was a slight sheen on her forehead from playing and the heat of the lights. She was beautiful. I rubbed her arm softly and smiled when her muscles jumped under my touch.

"I'm sorry I'm so sweaty. It's so hot onstage. I can't imagine what it would be like with a full house."

I watched her watch the performers. She laughed with

them and clapped for them. She had a healthy passion for music. I wanted that. I was sure that I had it at one point when I was much younger, but somewhere along the way my competitive drive got in the way of the art of music. I closed my eyes and focused on each instrument individually and how they paired together.

"What do you hear?" Hope asked.

I smiled. "I hear a great time." I was proud of my answer.

"That's not good enough. What else?" I felt her hand on my leg, resting above my knee, but below my thigh. I almost jumped at the contact, but the weight felt good and suppressed the shiver that threatened to bubble up.

I held my breath and focused. My eyes were still closed. "People are laughing, snapping their fingers, and clinking their glasses against other glasses. The bartender is talking to a waitress. I hear each instrument individually, and the melody as a whole. The saxophonist isn't as good as the woman who just played, but it's passable."

I felt Hope playfully nudge me with her shoulder. I opened my eyes.

"You're being sweet and kind. Charlie has been playing longer than I've been alive. Nobody plays the sax like he does."

He was really good, but I was wooing my girlfriend.

"He probably only plays the sax. You play everything and you teach." I was fierce about her and her ability. I was biased, but I loved her playing before I even knew the musician behind the music that touched me. Maybe I was ready to open up and feel it in my bones again, but she was the first to break through in over a decade, and that made her special.

Miles approached the table. "Hope, that was great. I'm so glad you came." He apologized for interrupting and asked if we were enjoying ourselves. Hope invited him to join us and he happily sat across from us. "Lily, do you play any instruments? Are you going to hit the stage tonight?"

I stared at him like deer in headlights.

"Lily's a wonderful music aficionado. She's been such a big help to me on the piano. She's actually very good with all instruments."

"Maybe she can help me with the trumpet. You know how much I struggle with that."

"You were great up there. You don't need any help." I was being truthful. Jazz was a forgiving genre, especially an impromptu jam session where it was more about respecting other musicians sharing the stage than one's own moment of glory. Solos were a thing for a reason.

"You know musicians are never happy with our performances." He laughed and reached out to squeeze my hand.

I didn't feel the need to draw back or recoil because his touch didn't bother me. As a matter of fact, it was encouraging. He made me want to play, too. What was happening to me? The walls that protected my former self were starting to crack. Hope knew exactly how to keep chipping away at their hardness. First herself, then the kids, now this. Blue Eden was a bar I would gladly frequent. Miles waved over three more drinks and spent a good half an hour sitting with us, telling fantastic tour stories of missing instruments and famous people he played with who encouraged him even more. To me, that was a sign a musician did their job, making inspiring music that was beautiful and changed lives. I'd like to think my music changed lives and maybe would again.

Hope flipped her wrist to check the time when Miles left us. My heart leapt in my chest. I knew what could happen tonight. I knew what I wanted to happen. I wanted to pick up where we left off, but truthfully, I was glad we had gone out.

"Are you ready to go?" I knew if I didn't ask, Hope wouldn't push. She knew my hangups and also knew I was enjoying myself.

"Only if you are."

She scooted out of the booth and reached for my hand. I didn't let her go until she said her good-byes in the form of hugs and kisses. I stood awkwardly at her side as people hugged me, too. Some people shook my hand instead, sensing I was standoffish and not entirely comfortable with their nearness.

"Spread the word, Hope. We will, too." Miles waved the stack of flyers Hope handed him when we arrived. "We'll be at the next concert. Maybe you and I can play a song or two."

I knew that would generate traffic for both the Leading Note and Blue Eden. I was excited to be a part of it and see how successful both businesses would be. Music. It was starting to become a thing for me again.

CHAPTER SEVENTEEN

That was so much fun. Really. Thank you."
She squeezed my hand playfully and tugged me toward her for a kiss.

"I'm glad you enjoyed it. That's the fun thing about jazz. A jam session like that doesn't have any structure, so you don't have to worry about missed notes or stumbles. It's so smooth, most people don't even know when there's a mistake."

The classical training in me couldn't help but notice, but it didn't bother me, surprisingly.

"What do you have in store for me now?" I held her wrist up to check the time.

"Let's hang out at my place for a bit. I'm still pumped up about tonight. But only if you want to. I know you probably want to get home to Clio."

I stopped her right there and kissed her. "Clio can wait. I've spoiled him too much over the last few years." I wasn't ready for this night to be over. I followed her up the stairs to her apartment and made myself comfortable on the couch.

"Again, I'm going to have to excuse myself for about ten minutes. I'm still hot from playing."

The last time she showered, she came out wearing tiny

shorts and a tank top. I was hoping for the same kind of luck. My anxiety ramped up when she left, so I paced into the kitchen and back to the living room, and panicked slightly when I heard a door open. I turned to find Hope wearing only a long cotton nightshirt that brushed the tops of her thighs. The light pink V-neck was loose enough to be comfortable, yet tight enough to show the shape of her body. Hope had curves and full breasts.

I swallowed hard and stared at her. I couldn't have imagined a more beautiful woman standing in front of me. The ends of her wet hair brushed across her nightshirt right below her hardened nipples. The thin material was virtually see-through where it was damp. She wasn't wearing anything underneath. I was frozen in place.

"You could have helped yourself to anything. Can I get you a drink?"

She placed her hand on my stomach as she walked by to head into the kitchen. I responded without thought. I reached out and pulled her against me. I cupped her face in my hands and kissed her. She moaned and moved close to me. When her body pushed up against mine, I lowered my hands to her hips and held her steady. Without breaking the kiss, she pulled me over to the couch, but I stopped her.

"Is there any way we can go into your room? I just mean because there is more space. I love that couch, don't get me wrong, but…"

Her kiss held a small, knowing smile that disappeared as she pulled me down the hall, touching me, slightly tugging at my clothes but giving me space to turn around if I needed to. I didn't even look around once she opened the door. My eyes were on Hope and the queen-size bed behind her. She crawled up on the bed once we reached the frame and reached out for me. I didn't hesitate. I followed her onto the bed until we were both on our sides facing one another.

"Are you okay?" Hope asked. She ran her fingertips delicately across my face and down my bare shoulder.

I shivered at how careful she was and the intensity I saw in her eyes. I nodded. I didn't want to talk. I leaned forward and kissed away the doubt and hesitation she had. I was ready for this moment. Dreamed about it my entire life. Even when I was young and didn't know what sex was, I knew there was intimacy. I trusted Hope with my heart and body.

"I want this. I want you. More than anything." There was no other place I wanted to be than right there.

Hope took my hand and moved it down her neck, ran it between the valley of her breasts and down to the soft folds between her thighs. My eyes widened when I felt her slick core. She rubbed my fingers up and down her slit, then moved them away. I understood what she wanted. She pushed into my hand, her back arched up, her breasts pressed against mine.

"Please, Lily."

That's all it took. I carefully slid inside her, completely in awe of how tight and smooth she felt. She moaned against my mouth when I found a nice rhythm. Hope was not shy. She spread her legs and thrust against my hand. I pulled back for a moment to slip a second finger in, but I was nervous and didn't want to hurt her. I fumbled around until she reached for my hand, brought it up to her mouth, and sucked on two fingers. Her warm mouth and swirling tongue wet them. I was never going to survive tonight.

"Now try."

I pushed inside her folds, into her warmth, and watched as her eyes fluttered shut. Her mouth dropped open. Her breath was hot against my cheek, and the moans and quick gasps that filled my ears were the best sounds I'd ever heard. I'd never created anything that sounded that beautiful until this very moment. I closed my eyes.

"I hear your sweet and sexy noises deep in the back of your throat," I said.

Her hand slid up my arm to touch my cheek. She ran her fingertips over my face and rested against my lips. I placed a soft kiss against her fingers.

"What else do you hear?" Her voice was hoarse and deep.

I shivered as her fingers ran down my throat and across my collarbone. "I hear my heartbeat pounding. It's so fast." I lowered my voice out of embarrassment because I'd never said anything like my next words. "I can hear how wet you are for me."

She moaned at that and spread her legs even wider. In my mind, in my fantasies, my first time was supposed to be flowers and candles. Instead, we had the lights on, were on top of the covers, and we both had clothes on. It was so different, and yet just as perfect.

"Can I touch you?" she asked.

I looked at her and almost cried at her sincerity. I slowly pulled out of her, leaned up, and stripped off my dress. The light blue lacy bra and matching panties weren't top-of-the-line sexy, but they made me feel feminine and beautiful. I wanted Hope to see me and want me as much as I wanted her.

"I'm all yours."

She leaned up on her elbows to look at me.

I was completely self-conscious, and it took great effort to not turn off the light or cross my arms over my chest.

She ran her hand down my side and across my stomach. "You're softer than I imagined. So very pretty and pure."

I watched her fingertips glide across my quivering abdomen and up to the bare skin above my small breasts.

"So perfect," she said as she openly stared at me. Just

when I thought she was moving closer, she climbed off the bed, turned off the overhead light, and turned on a light on the nightstand.

Before I even had a chance to relax with the darkened room, Hope slipped off her nightshirt and walked over to me, gloriously naked. I didn't even try masking my appreciation. She pulled back the covers but stopped me from climbing into their safety.

"Can I stare at you, just for a moment? If you don't mind? I want to remember this night. You are so beautiful, Lily. I wish you could see yourself. The way your hair is pulled over your shoulder, and you have the most adorable tendrils framing your face." She looked at my breasts and down to my matching panties. "And light blue is definitely my favorite color. As of today."

The Chicago summer night didn't care what was happening on the third floor of the 203 Scott building. Nobody but the two of us knew how special this moment was. Hope never pushed me or tried to speed things up. My respect for her grew by leaps and bounds every time she slowed life down for me.

"Your cheeks get rosy when we kiss. And this body?" She looked me over several times before continuing. "Stunning really."

I reached for her. I needed her body against mine. I needed to feel her close and to cover up my discomfort. Hope was the first person to see me this way. The starkness of my near nakedness was overwhelming. She came to me, wrapped me in her arms, and waited for me to adjust to the newness of us. When she kissed me, she did it softly, yet fiercely. I felt safe in her arms. My stomach still quivered, but a calm washed over me when I looked into her eyes. I trusted her. She was the first person I completely trusted as an adult. I put space between us only so I could unclasp my bra. I was ready for her hands all over me.

"Touch me."

It was more of a croaked whisper than the sexy voice I wanted to project. I cleared my throat to repeat myself, but she silenced me with another one of her mind-numbing kisses. Her tongue touched mine softly at first, then plunged deeply inside my mouth. It was erotic, demanding, and made me weak. I felt her fingertips slip underneath the bra straps and slide them off my shoulders. Her hard nipples pressed into mine and I moaned at the intimacy of our skin touching. She stopped.

"Is this okay?"

"Definitely," I said.

Chills raced across my body under her fingertips. Her touch was soft and arousing. She made sure I was looking at her when her fingers cupped my breast for the first time. The feeling of her warm hand against my vulnerable skin made me shiver. Different emotions swirled inside me, but not once did I feel overwhelmed by them. Loved, treasured, exhilarated, frightened of the unknown, thrilled at the moment, but not overwhelmed. Her hands were so warm and my nipples were already painfully erect, but her fingers massaged away the discomfort and replaced it with need. I needed her to touch me. My blood was racing, warming with every beat. Her hand slid down to my panties, already slick with want, and slipped inside them. We both moaned as she rubbed my swollen center, back and forth, the pressure of her palm right on my clit. I leaned forward with weakness.

"Let's lie down," she said.

I happily obliged. She pulled the thin floral sheet over us to give me some warmth. I was shaking for an entirely different reason, not because I was cold. Hope slid one of her legs between mine and rolled on top of me. She kissed my neck, my cheek, my collarbone and worked her way down to my breasts. I resisted wrapping my hands in her hair, so I rested them on her shoulders instead. She was sweet and gentle, and when she sucked my nipple in her mouth, I arched into her. The shock of how good it felt was amazing. My hands found the back of her head and held her in place. I wanted to keep feeling this good. My body responded the same way when she reached my other nipple. I hissed and moaned and writhed beneath her. My hands ran down her body, and before I realized what I was doing, I was cupping her ass and pulling her against me. I should have been embarrassed, but I didn't care. My body was on fire, and I needed to ease this ache.

Hope reached down and, after a quick nod from me, pulled my panties off. We were both naked. Everything after that was a blur. Her hands were all over me and I loved every touch. She looked into my eyes, kissed me softly, and slid inside me. I opened my mouth and exhaled in surprise. When I did it to myself, it didn't feel like this. It didn't take my breath away or feel so intimate.

She moved slowly, but I wanted more of her. I moved my hips against her hand. The deeper she went, the higher my hips greeted her. Her mouth abandoned mine and moved down my body. I almost jumped up when her warm tongue touched my clit. It was so raw and perfect. Emotionally, I was higher than I'd ever been, and physically I was getting ready to crash. Hope knew exactly what I liked. She massaged my slit with her wet mouth while her finger slid in and out.

My head rolled from side to side and I begged her to make me come. Words I'd never said flew out of my mouth, demanding this or that. The more assertive she was with me, the louder I got. When I finally came, I tensed up and released in a single shout. I curled in a ball as the aftershocks rocked my body with tiny pleasurable explosions. Hope held me and pulled the covers over us. Her heartbeat was thunderous in her chest, or maybe that was mine. I honestly had no idea.

"Thank you," she whispered against my forehead. She hugged me closer to her.

I knew what she was thanking me for, but she didn't need to. I hated that I started crying. Tonight was another breakthrough for me. Having so many back to back was exhausting.

"Hey, hey. It's okay. It's okay."

That only made me cry harder. "No, I'm sorry. Tonight has been wonderful. Really. I just never knew it could be like this."

There was a low rumble in her chest as she cleared her throat. "So, all of this was good? I didn't do anything that you didn't like?"

I leaned up to look at her. She brushed away a tear with the pad of her thumb. She smelled like me. I kissed her fingers.

"It was perfect and I loved everything. Thank you for being gentle with me. Always, actually. You have helped me so much these past few months, more than you will ever know." I teared up again, but didn't look away. "Wait. Are you crying now?"

Hope laughed as a few tears fell out of the corners of her eyes. "Yes. I am. This was so special for me, too." She reached up and kissed me hard. I tasted myself on her lips and realized this night was far from over.

I had a naked beautiful woman in my arms, and even though it was well after midnight, neither one of us was ready to sleep. I touched her breast and marveled at how responsive her body was. She placed her hand over mine and squeezed until she moaned with pleasure. Hope was great at sharing what she liked and what she wanted.

"Oh, God." She was so wet when I slid inside her again that I couldn't keep quiet. I was amazed at her body and how well it reacted to my touch. She was grabbing me from the inside, hungrily, wanting more and more.

"Faster, Lily," she said.

Her gasps and moans were intoxicating. She licked the tip of her finger and slid her hand between our bodies. When I realized she was massaging her clit at the same time I was slamming into her, I kissed her. I put every emotion into that kiss to let her know how I felt about her and about tonight. She cried out against my lips when her orgasm overtook her. I was in awe at the way her center quivered and pulsated around my fingers. I'd never even felt my own body during an orgasm. It was life changing.

"I want to stay inside you forever." I buried my face in the soft spot on the side of her neck.

She lifted my chin so that I would look at her. "I'm okay with that." The honesty I saw in her expression made my eyes well up.

"Don't cry. Don't cry."

I willed myself to think about anything other than this moment. I wanted to be strong our first time, and so far I'd been a quivering mess.

"You have incredibly strong hands." She brought my fingers to her mouth to place tiny kisses on each fingertip. She didn't know that it was because I had played piano and other instruments every single day for half of my life.

"I type a lot." Lame, but this moment was serious and I didn't want to think about my past. I wanted to stay in this bliss for as long as possible. I rested my head on her shoulder as she played with my hair and told me why tonight was her favorite night.

"We should probably try to get some sleep," she said. I

looked at the clock. It was almost four. "If you fall asleep now, you still have time to dream."

I lazily stroked the curvy underside of her breast and played with a tiny mole near her rib cage. "Why? My dream is right here with you."

CHAPTER EIGHTEEN

Hey, sleepyhead. It's almost noon. Clio called. He wants us to bring over cheese. And dessert since it's so late."

Hope kissed me on the cheek. I cracked open an eye and found a smiling Hope sitting beside me on the bed. She set a steaming cup of coffee on the nightstand for me. I crawled back under the covers. She followed me and kissed every part of my body until I was completely awake and laughing with her.

"Hi." I felt shy and a complete mess. I tried patting down my hair, but it was a curly mop and out of control. I shrugged.

"Hi. Are you ready for this day?" She leaned forward and kissed me. "I was hungry and I wanted to make you breakfast in bed, but then morning turned to the afternoon and I realized I didn't have any food here. Rather than leave, I thought I'd check to see if you wanted to grab lunch somewhere. Or I could go pick something up if you wanted to shower and stay relaxed and beautiful in my bed."

I felt the rush of blood hit all of my sensitive spots just remembering the last twelve hours of my life. That I was even able to look Hope in the eye was remarkable. "A shower sounds fantastic."

"Okay, why don't I run across the street and pick us up

some lunch while you shower. There are fresh towels in the bathroom and you should find anything you need in there as well. Including a brush." She winked at me as my hands automatically went up to my unruly hair. Placing a quick kiss on my lips, she left me alone.

I didn't get out of bed until I heard the front door close and lock. I jumped up and raced to the bathroom. I didn't look any different. My hair was out of control, but that was expected. My skin was warm and my cheeks were flushed with the excitement and the newness of being in love. There were a few marks on my body that weren't there before last night that made me smile at myself in the mirror. I felt like a new person. I felt like a woman.

I turned on the shower and jumped in. Hope had left a new toothbrush, a hairbrush, and a folded pile of her clothes on the vanity that I assumed were for me. Her soap, her shampoo, even the apricot baby oil made me smile and think of her. I rushed because I knew she wasn't going to be gone long. When I walked into the living room after my shower, I found Hope arranging lunch.

In the light of day, after sleep and being apart for thirty minutes, I was shy all over again. "Thanks. And thanks for putting out clothes for me." I looked down at the cute oversized T-shirt and shorts. She was definitely curvier, but I appreciated the gesture and the fresh clothes.

"Come here," she said. I cleared my throat and forced myself to make eye contact with her as I crossed the room. She reached out and pulled me close. "I like the way you look in my clothes. Just like how I like the way you look in my bed."

I felt myself blush. She kissed me softly, and it escalated quickly. It was as if our lips were never apart. Our chemistry was remarkable. Or maybe it was just the newness of our changed relationship.

"What's for lunch?" I was too embarrassed to talk about our early morning and she was respectful enough not to push.

"I picked up a few salads and a meatball sub. I know I'm hungry this morning, but I also know how much you like salads."

I stopped myself from rolling my eyes. Nobody liked salads, but they were a necessary evil to stay trim. The meatball sub had my interest. I sat down, as directed by Hope, and took a long drink of the ice water she had put out for us.

"Thank you for getting this for us. I'm sorry I slept in. Usually I'm on a better schedule." I looked down at my plate and played with my silverware. Was the morning after always this awkward for people?

"It's the weekend. There are no schedules on the weekends. I don't want to assume you are free this afternoon, but if you are, I'd love to spend it with you."

How did I manage to find the perfect girlfriend? She always knew what to say, when to back off, when to push me, when to encourage me, and when to protect me. I was still rattled by the guy who had approached me at the museum. Hope was my champion and had completely shut him down in seconds, but did so in such a polite manner.

"I'm all yours." Then I blushed, realizing what I said. She winked at me. I blushed harder, but smiled this time. I was good with an afternoon in bed.

"Let's go back to your place. That way we can bring Clio a meatball and he'll quit calling me."

"You're sweet to think of my boy." I felt bad because I knew Clio was going to be mad at me for only having kibble to eat, but he wasn't going to starve. I could have stayed here all day. Maybe even convinced Hope to play different instruments for me. But I didn't want to be demanding. I just wanted time with her.

We cleaned up the dining room together, the activity stretching longer than it should have because we were in close proximity and had a hard time keeping our hands to ourselves. She would softly squeeze my hip as she brushed by me or kiss my shoulder when I scooted in front of her. Having a small kitchen was beneficial for makeout sessions.

"Ready?" Hope gave me a bag to stash my dress in.

The sandals she gave me were a bit snug, but wearing tall heels with a T-shirt and shorts was not a good fashion statement. She reached for my hand and we headed down to the train station. There was no walk of shame. I felt invigorated and wondered if the world noticed anything different about me today. Correction. I wondered if the world even noticed me today. I noticed it for the first time in a long time.

❖

"Don't hate me, boy." Clio grumbled as he sauntered away from me when we walked into my condo. He stopped when Hope rattled the paper bag that held the meatball and turned back when she opened it up and he got a whiff of it. Ignoring me, he walked straight up to Hope and rubbed all over her legs. "Oh, suddenly now you're going to be sweet? Now that Hope brings you food?" His meow was innocent enough. I handed Hope his dish. "Just drop it in. He likes to tear into it."

"How long has he been with you again?" She bravely petted his head while he attacked the meatball.

"A little over two years." My heart softened when I thought about his first day with me. He was a mess, but he let me clean him up and we got over one another's hesitancy. I thought we were close until I saw how gentle he was with Hope. He loved her more than he loved me. Jerk. "I'm going to slip into my own clothes, if you don't mind." How I survived the trip wearing sandals that were too small for me was a mystery. I kicked them off the second we walked into my place. I retreated to my bedroom, grabbed a skirt, a top, and fresh underwear and headed to the en suite bathroom. I quickly dressed and pulled my hair up into a bun. The humidity was frizzing it beyond help. Product wouldn't help, and I honestly didn't want to be away from Hope too long. I missed her.

I walked back into my bedroom and found Hope curled up on my bed, a small pillow clutched in her arm. My heart nearly catapulted out of my chest. No woman had been in my bedroom before. I fumbled at words until something coherent fell out.

"I wanted to see your bedroom. You should think about putting up a painting or a series of photographs in here."

"Um, yeah, I know. I need art for all of my walls. My place is super boring, especially compared to yours." I sat on the edge of the bed and played with the lacy comforter.

She crawled over to me. "Do we need to leave this room?"

I tried really hard not to look down at her cleavage. I wanted to keep eye contact with her and talk about anything but what was on my mind. I failed. The lure of her body and everything that happened between us won out. I surprised us both by reaching down and running my fingertip over the soft, creamy exposed skin.

"I have little marks on my body," I said.

She sat up. "I'm so sorry, Lily. I didn't mean to—" She stopped talking when I put my finger against her lips.

"I wasn't complaining. I actually liked it. It was nice to lose myself with you."

She leaned up and kissed my neck softly. "I liked losing myself with you, too. It was a wonderful night, or morning. One that I will never forget." She nipped lightly at my jaw and

I shivered. "Are you okay with this? I just don't know what you like yet and what you don't like."

I almost snorted. There wasn't anything she did that was uncomfortable. I was the bumbling idiot who didn't know anything about pleasing a woman.

"Everything was nice." That was a horrible word choice. I shook my head. "Not nice."

"It wasn't nice?" She feigned hurt. She was teasing me and knew full well I was struggling.

"No, it was great. It was better than nice. So much better. I guess I'm trying to tell you that it was incredible. I'm happy and fortunate that it was with you. My first time." I ducked my head because I was beyond embarrassed. I was mortified. I'd never had such an intimate conversation before, not even with my therapist.

"Hey, come here." Hope put her arms around me. "Listen to me. You were amazing and incredible, and I would have never known that it was your first time. I mean, I knew, but you did everything right and just the way I like it." She made me look at her and nodded to reaffirm her words. She kissed me. It was soft and sweet, and within seconds, I was flat on my back. She didn't rush me, and even though I wanted to shed the clothes I just put on, I knew we had all afternoon and evening to just be us. We scooted so our heads rested on the pillows. Hope leaned up on her elbow and ran her fingertips up and down my arm. Chills exploded across half of my body.

"You are so gentle with me," I said.

When her fingers brushed across my neck and over to the other side, I closed my eyes. I could get used to Hope touching me.

"You are very responsive to touch. It's nice."

"I'm very responsive to your touch." I emphasized "your"

because I wasn't a touchy-feely person. Even hugs were new to me.

Her caresses grew bolder. She unbuttoned the second button on my blouse to expose more skin. "Let's play a game."

I quirked an eyebrow at her. I was intrigued. I never played games, but a game in my bedroom? I had a feeling I was going to like this one. A lot. "Okay. Tell me the game and the rules."

"I haven't decided what it's called yet, but the rules are fun. Every inch of skin that's exposed, I touch."

I refrained from tearing off my clothes. "I think I'm going to like this game. Is it your turn?"

"It is my turn. Close your eyes."

She drew circles on my arm, around my neck, and up to my face. I slightly puckered my lips when her fingers brushed over them. I heard her smile. The bedroom was extremely quiet. I heard her breathing, lazy Sunday traffic, Clio's bowl clinking against the baseboard as he tried to get more out of it than was there, and the soft hum of the air conditioner blowing cold air into the room.

Her fingers stalled at the second button. I reached up and unbuttoned the third one, then the fourth. She moved back up to my neck and down my other arm. I could smell her sweet perfume and shampoo as she leaned over to reach my other arm. Her hair brushed across my chest, the silkiness of her waves as soft as her caresses. I reached down and untucked the blouse from my skirt and finished opening the rest of the buttons. She moaned in appreciation. I cracked open my eyes.

"No peeking." She furrowed her brows in fake reprimand. I smiled and closed them again. I felt the bed wobble and gasped slightly when I felt her straddle me. Both warm hands pressed against my stomach and ran upward until my bra hindered any further movement. She stopped and waited. I reached up and unclasped the tiny hook in front. My bra bounced open a little bit, but still covered my breasts. She twirled her fingers around the lace until I got the hint and pulled it completely away from my body. I tried not to think of how exposed I was, but when both hands cupped me, I didn't care. I moaned at her gentle massage. My nipples instantly hardened at her touch. Every single part of my breast was sensitive. I felt her hair on my stomach and chest as she bent to kiss my nipple, but stopped short.

"What's wrong?" I asked after several seconds of no movement from her. I opened my eyes and looked at her. She sat back up.

"This is a touching game only. I almost forgot."

"Technically, your mouth would be touching my body, so I think that works in the rules." I was pleading with her. She cocked her head to the side to contemplate what I was saying. She shook her head.

"No. I don't think we can change the rules now. We already started."

I groaned and fell back on the pillow. She leaned back and touched my calves. The game was back on.

"We seem to be in a quandary. You're on my skirt, so I can't take it off." I tried to shrug as nonchalantly as I could with my blouse open and my bra undone. "I guess the game is over. How sad."

She chuckled and climbed off me. "Oh, I don't think it's over. I think I'm just learning the loopholes." She leaned back on her elbow and stroked my calves and knees.

I pulled my skirt up to mid-thigh.

"Why are your eyes open?"

I shut them immediately. I moaned when she touched the sensitive skin on the sides of my knees and ran her fingertips up my thighs until they reached the hem. It was going to have to come off. I tilted my pelvis up and awkwardly unzipped it. I fell back on the bed and casually shimmied it down my thighs. I wasn't even done kicking it off before I felt her fingers on my thighs. I stopped my movements because I needed her touch there. I spread my legs as far as I could with a skirt trapping my knees.

"You are deliberately making it hard to play this game," she said.

I decided to play along. Like this was an inconvenience for me, too. "I don't believe you've touched me everywhere yet." I had no idea where this confidence was coming from since just a few hours ago, I couldn't look her in the eye.

"Roll over."

I opened my eyes at that command.

"What?"

"You heard me. Roll over."

Suddenly, I was nervous. It must have shown on my face because Hope instantly backed off.

"You don't have to. I'm sorry. I'm pushing too fast."

I flipped over, slipped out of my blouse, and discarded my bra. I felt ridiculous because I didn't kick off my skirt. I was still trapped. I dropped my head on the pillow and groaned. I couldn't even imagine the view Hope had of me. Bare back, pink panties, and a wrinkled skirt wrapped around my knees. A part of me wanted to panic, but once I felt Hope's soft touch against my back, my panic turned into a fluttering, pleasant feeling that relaxed me and excited me at the same time. I was never going to get used to the up-and-down feelings I experienced with Hope. She massaged, scratched, and then caressed me into a submissive, relaxed woman. When she tugged to pull my skirt off, I didn't remind her the game was still on. We both knew it was over.

When I felt her lips on my shoulder, I shuddered as

pleasure ripped through my body. I was sensitive everywhere. She straddled me again and touched and kissed all over my back. The soft area under my shoulder blade made me gasp. I smiled when I felt her lips press twice against my lower back, right above my panties.

"I love, love these sexy dimples."

I had dimples there? She dipped her finger into the band of my panties and rolled them down, exposing the top of my ass. She kissed me there, too. I stiffened at the newness. She felt my hesitation and flipped me again.

"We'll save that for another time." We will? I had no idea what she meant. "You're so beautiful, Lily. And you're mine." She covered my body with hers and stretched my arms above my head.

Feeling her on top of me sent my pulse racing. She kissed me deeply and pressed herself into me. I spread my legs to accommodate her and ended up wrapping them against her waist as she rolled her hips into me. A heat blossomed inside me and made my entire body feel like it was on fire. This was a different feeling than I had earlier this morning. I pulled off Hope's shirt. Our lips separated enough to get it over her head, then reconnected immediately. How I ended up in a sitting position with Hope on my lap, I didn't know, but I liked it. I reached behind her and unlatched her bra. Hope had beautiful breasts and I wanted to feel them again. Taste them again.

She unpinned my hair and shook it loose. "You should always wear your hair down. It gives you a wild, sexy look that drives me crazy."

Noted. I would throw away all hair ties the second she left. She wrapped her hands in my hair and brought her breast to my lips. I didn't hesitate. I sucked her into my mouth and swirled my tongue around her nipple.

"Harder." She moaned. She gasped when I increased the pressure and groaned when she felt the tops of my teeth gently scrape her skin. "Yes, just like that." She unbuttoned her pants.

My hands slid to her hips and I pulled her toward me. It was impossible to touch her because her clothes were in the way. She jumped off me to slip out of the rest of her clothes and was back on my lap in seconds. Fuck. My panties were still on. One day I would be good at this. Not today.

CHAPTER NINETEEN

W as your day as crazy as mine?" Hope sounded drained. I was still on a high from my weekend with her. When my boss emailed me a shitty account, I thanked him and started researching. Nothing was going to break my good mood. "It was busy, but not over the top. What's going on there?"

"The same stuff. Hitting up businesses for donations. For some reason, it was easier in our old building. Since we've moved, we've lost quite a bit of funds. My brother's company was a big blow to our bottom dollar. I shouldn't complain. We got a low-rent place for a year." She sounded dejected. She'd already refused to take any money from me. I was already planning on making an anonymous donation, but I just needed to free up some of my CDs. If she didn't know I was the one donating, it couldn't change our relationship dynamics.

"What about corporate level? Big companies set aside money for exactly this kind of thing. I know you are trying to keep it local, but corporations are a part of local communities whether people like it or not. If I'm out of line, please let me know. I'm just trying to brainstorm with you." Hope D'Marco knew how to do her job. I was a nobody giving her advice on something I didn't need to.

"No, no. You're right. I love saying locally sponsored, but I would hate to say we are closing. It might be a long shot and I might have sat on it too long."

I sent an email to my banker requesting money in a cashier's check while Hope chatted about the different companies she could try. I could pick up the check by the end of the week and slip it to Agnes and tell her not to let Hope know it was from me. I'd send a courier, but a fifty-thousand-dollar cashier's check was something that had to be done in person. I knew I could donate as Jillian Crest, but she had disappeared over a decade ago. Resurfacing to donate that kind of money would only generate more focus on her. I couldn't handle that kind of scrutiny. I also sent my boss an email about the organization and encouraged him to donate. I knew he would get it to the right people and probably donate some money, too. Hope was still talking.

"Am I interrupting you? I can hear you typing. I'm sorry. I'll let you go," she said.

"No, I'm sorry. That was rude. I'm done. I'm all yours."

"I remember the last time you said that to me."

I blushed instantly. I remembered it, too. Vividly. And I wanted to relive it. Over and over. I was braver with Hope yesterday. She gave me full permission to touch her anywhere and try anything I wanted. She was patient and respectful with me. I tried not to think about her past lovers and what things they did to her. My inexperience made me feel pathetic, but she never made me feel inadequate.

"When do I get to see you again?" I rolled my eyes at my own impatience. I refused to be like Carrie in college who wouldn't let me have any peace and quiet. "I mean, I know this is a busy week for you, but will you be free any night? Maybe we can go to dinner?" I really wanted her to come over and make out with me, but I didn't know how to say that without sounding desperate.

"Dinner would be nice. How about Wednesday night? Does that work for you?"

"Let me check my busy social calendar," I said.

She laughed. The deep throaty sounds sent shivers down my spine. "You're opening up quite nicely. I wouldn't be surprised if you didn't already have something else lined up. Isn't Wednesday pool night at Bleachers?"

I forgot all about that. Josh sent me a few text messages reminding me that they could always use me on the team and join them anytime I wanted. "I can meet with them anytime. I want to see you."

"I would like that very much. I miss you already."

I got giddy and tried hard not to giggle like a little girl. "I miss you, too. I'll think about places we can eat and get back to you."

"Or I could just bring dinner over. I like your place. And I love Clio," Hope said.

"We would both love that. Okay, get back to work. Text me later if you want."

I finally understood the need to be around somebody you loved all of the time. It really was a need. My body, my heart, and my mind wanted to be near her. Since I met Hope two months ago, I hadn't had a single nightmare, but had several life-changing moments. I always had nightmares if my routine changed at all, even if the changes were good. I fell in love for the first time, I had sex for the first time, I went to a bar with live music for the first time, and only had dreamless nights since I met Hope, which suited me fine. Dr. Monroe had been trying to break me out of my comfort zone for years, but Hope showed me how. Because of her, the idea of hanging out with my colleagues at a bar suddenly wasn't so scary, even if she wasn't there to hold my hand. I guess I just thought shutting myself off from the world for the rest of my life was the answer. I was wrong. Climbing out of this hole was going to take a lot of time and patience.

I stopped working at seven. I pictured Hope still sitting at her desk, expanding her reach to businesses outside of the Chicago area. She was determined. The Leading Note was her dream. I wasn't sure how much difference my donation would make, but I hoped it would give the center a breather for a bit. Hope had mentioned she didn't want to stay where they were, but there were so many restoration projects around town that property values were skyrocketing and it was hard to find a safe, cheap place for them near any school or residential area. Chicago had an interesting layout. I lived in Hyde Park, but almost everybody there could afford private lessons for their children and the Leading Note wouldn't thrive. Plus, the rent for an organization like the Leading Note would be staggering. Hope needed to find an area that needed her as much as she needed it.

"Clio, do you want Italian or Chinese tonight?"

He yawned at me. I was indecisive, too. I finally made a decision, placed the order on my phone app, and sat on the couch. I was exhausted. The weekend had been crazy, incredible, and indescribable. I worked late tonight only because I had to do everything twice because I couldn't concentrate. I could only think of Hope. Even when she wasn't here, she was in my heart, and that gave me strength. I turned on the TV to the music stations and pulled up old-time jazz. The music I'd heard in the stores Saturday, mainstream stuff, was horrible. I decided I hadn't missed much with popular music. I was curious about Miles and his musical history. I would Google him later. Right then, I had zero energy to do anything but sit on the couch and listen to music. When Miles had asked me if I was going to play onstage with them, panic set in, but it wasn't the bad kind. Since meeting Hope, I'd discovered a different kind of panic. It was the kind that made my heart beat faster and my palms sweat, but I didn't need to run away. I'd never participated in a jam session before. And I think if I had practiced any instrument, and maybe after I knew everybody a little bit better, I might have done it.

The doorbell interrupted my fantasy. I buzzed Ryan up and waited at the door. I liked Ryan. He was nice but wasn't over-the-top friendly. He was there to do his job and do it well. I tipped him more because he understood me. Our exchange at the door took three seconds. The breadsticks smelled wonderful. I prepped a plate of angel hair, Alfredo with a dash of pesto, and a breadstick.

I retreated to my computer and looked up Miles Brand on Google and then YouTube. Surprisingly, he didn't start playing until he was fifteen. I listened to several clips that fans had uploaded. I hated bad recordings because you missed the subtleness between notes. Some musicians wanted to make that distinction, which I always found distracting, so whenever I heard somebody play who was smooth, it always caught my ear.

As much as I wanted to Google myself, I couldn't do it. I knew the most watched clip was going to be my meltdown onstage or the first time I conducted. An eleven-year-old conductor. I smiled. I barely remembered it, but I do remember the looks on the faces of the orchestra. Most of their faces were pinched with disdain. Only a few took me seriously. They especially didn't like it when I gave them advice. An eleven-year-old couldn't possibly master anything. I moved on from that memory. I punched in Hope's name and was surprised by everything that popped up. There were several interviews about the Leading Note and the push for community awareness and involvement. Hope looked young, eager, and excited. She was still all of those, but heavy doses of reality had jaded her somewhat. The world wasn't as giving as we all wanted.

I'm eating a salad. What did you have for dinner?

I smiled when her name popped up on my phone.

I ate fattening, cheesy Italian food. And bread. Yum.

Jealous. I did put a lot of salad dressing on these greens. And lots of cheese. I think at this point, it's no longer healthy.

I wanted to call her. I missed her voice. When she was tired, her voice got lower and raspier. I refrained, though. The only good thing to come from my relationship with Carrie from college was that she taught me everything not to do in a relationship.

Clio would so be your best friend right now. I gave him a noodle but he couldn't have cared less.

I should have felt bad that I was using Clio to keep the conversation going, but he was a safe topic that didn't have me saying awkward things to her. And I was close to being needy. Wednesday was forty-eight hours away. I could do it. I did it for years. Except this time, I didn't want to hide. I didn't want the world to forget about me. Correction. I didn't want Hope to forget about me.

I'm glad I'm not allergic to him.

That's because I sanitize my entire place before you come over.

Do you really? That makes me sad.

I wrote, *You know I would do anything to make you feel comfortable*, but then I deleted it because that was creepy. I tried again. *You know I just want you to feel comfortable.* Texting was the better form of communication for me because it gave me time to think. My track record with Hope and stupid things I'd said wasn't the greatest. As a matter of fact, some of the things I said still made me cringe. Maybe I did need to hang out at Bleachers because the gang there would help me socialize without even knowing it. Josh knew I was quiet, he just didn't know why.

You are the sweetest person. Hope always knew what to say. How did I get so lucky?

Where are you now?

I'm on the L headed home. I grabbed a salad from across the street. I plan on taking a hot bath and going to bed early. Mondays always exhaust me.

I really wanted to say something cutesy or even slightly sexual, but I had no idea how to be flirtatious without sounding creepy.

Relax, rest, and think of me. There. That wasn't bad. I stared at the phone a few minutes before I realized she wasn't going to text back. She probably reached her stop and was on her way home. I put down the phone and started researching my own company and B&T and where they stood on charitable contributions. Even if Hope didn't want my money, she would probably be okay taking it from Corporate America.

Chapter Twenty

"How are you with water?" It was the Wednesday after another fantastically sexual weekend with Hope. I called her because I wanted to actually get out of the condo and maybe do something for her like spend the weekend at Lake Geneva. I found a really nice hotel on the water that offered fun boating activities and had a very romantic package for couples. It was cheesy, but Hope was the kind of woman who appreciated the effort.

"I love showers and baths. Can you be a little more specific?"

"I wanted to take you away for the weekend. And I just remembered I don't have a license, so you might have to drive." I was such an idiot for not thinking ahead.

Hope playfully laughed at me. "I can rent a car and we can go wherever you want, but we'd have to leave either late Friday night or early Saturday. I just scheduled a seven o'clock session."

I tried not to let it bother me, especially since it was a music therapy session. I had quickly figured out she said "session" for a therapy patient and "lesson" for a student. Hope dropped everything when she worked with patients and

I didn't blame her one bit. My two-minute session with Kylie was so exhilarating, and her response had melted me.

"That's fine. I just want to get you out and away from my condo. I feel like I'm keeping you there for selfish reasons and you deserve so much more," I said.

"You're kidding, right? Lily, I love spending time with you and making love and laughing and sleeping and eating and being around you. You are my girlfriend. We are a new couple. Getting to know one another the way we have is my dream come true."

I felt the smile on my face grow. "Are you sure? I don't want you to get bored with me or us or not have a good time because of my anxiety issues."

"How about this? I pack a bag, head to your place Friday night, and we don't go outside until Sunday late morning when I have to wake you up and beg you to take me to brunch. I'll bring over movies, you get groceries to hold us over until then, and we'll spend the entire time in bed or on the couch."

I took a deep breath and held it. It was the perfect plan. My heart filled my entire body with happiness and threatened to burst outside of my body. I exhaled slowly to give myself time to settle.

"I think that is a great idea." See? Mature.

"Please breathe. I still need you."

I exhaled the second breath I held. I didn't realize she could hear me and felt foolish. "See? You make me do weird things."

"You were weird when I first met you. Weird and wonderful. That's why I lo—like you so much."

She was still talking, but the only thing I could hear was my own thick heartbeat resonating in my head. She'd almost said "love." I heard it. I stood up and paced. I had to play it cool, though.

"Are you still there?" Hope asked.

"Oh, yes. I'm here. Sorry. My mind wandered." *Yes, it wandered right to your heart and poked around, hoping you would say the word to me.* There was no way I could tell her that I loved her. It was too soon. This wasn't a romance novel. This was real life, and what worked on the page didn't work for me.

"Is that okay?"

I sat down and tapped my foot. "Of course that's okay. Will you bring your saxophone and play for me, too? I miss hearing you play."

"I'm sad you aren't working around here. I miss your ear and your advice. You should come here and give me a lesson."

I froze, not because it was a bad idea, but because it was a good one. Now was the time to come clean. I could go up there, listen to her play, give her advice, and maybe, just maybe, tell her about Jillian Crest.

"I'll be there in an hour." I disconnected the phone and stared at it in my hand, afraid she would call back, but she didn't. I was committed. Fuck.

❖

Even though I was stressed, being back at the Leading Note felt good. I could hear music coming from inside. I sat on the stairs outside and listened. There were a few musicians playing, probably getting ready for the concert next week. Chicago summers were brutal and I didn't want a sunburn, so I reluctantly went inside. The second I saw Agnes, I groaned. I'd forgotten to swing by the bank and get the check. I would do that and bring it by Monday. I sent a quick text to my banker and asked him to hold it for me until then.

"You really did show up. What a nice surprise," Hope

said. She followed a few students down the stairs and told them she would see them tomorrow. When she turned to look at me, my knees wobbled. How was this wonderful woman mine? She leaned into me and kissed me softly after the kids left the building. "Hi, you."

"Mmm. Hi." I was ready to take her up to her office and fulfill any promise I made concerning why I stopped by. I sighed when she stepped away.

"I'm still on the clock. Come on. I want you to listen to something."

Her moans, her wet center, her short breaths, all sounds I would love to hear right then. "What were you thinking of playing?"

"You tell me, okay?"

I nervously followed her into the room. My anxiety started gaining strength as I got closer to the piano. I sat in the second row.

"What are you doing all the way over there? Come sit next to me." She pouted when I shook my head. "Why not?"

All of the reasons rushed up and sat in my throat, waiting for me to push them out, but I couldn't. This was going to have to be done in baby steps. She already called me weird. I didn't want to slip any further down her list. "I can hear better when I'm not so close. Does that make sense?" It didn't to me, but I hoped she thought it was just one of my quirks and shrugged it off.

"I'm nervous. I've only played this a few times. I'm still getting used to it." She rubbed her hands on her jeans, then blew on her fingers. "Ready?"

When the notes to Chopin-Liszt's "Meine Freuden" started, all of my repressed emotions about music rushed to the surface. They knocked down my walls and hovered between me and Hope. I clutched a book I found on the chair next to me and told myself to calm down. I was there to help and guide, not relive my past. This was my girlfriend who asked for my help. She didn't know about my internal struggles about music. She only knew I was a great listener and had helped her before.

"Relax, relax, relax. Enjoy it," I repeated until I actually started listening to the music. The tension in my shoulders dissipated and I closed my eyes and blew out the breath I'd been holding since Hope started playing. It was a very ambitious piece and she was doing a great job. She was warmed up nicely from her previous lessons, and it was nice to hear her interpretation of the music. I found that I didn't want to correct her. Hope's pauses were nice and fluid. Transitions were so important for the emotional responses, and if timed just right, you could bring an entire audience to tears. I discreetly brushed mine away. She was still learning and memorizing the piece, so some pauses were forgiven, but some were brilliantly timed. When she finished, the stillness in the room was deafening. When she finally made eye contact with me, I looked away. I was moved too much by it. I leaned my head back and looked up at the ceiling.

"That was very good, Hope."

"Any pointers for me?"

I still couldn't look at her. I closed my eyes and replayed it from memory. "Not really. I think once the piece is completely memorized, then you can work on breaks and timing, but you played it beautifully." I was exhausted.

"I wish my fingers were longer. I would be able to reach the keys effortlessly. You are so lucky. You have long, strong fingers."

I finally looked at her. The look she gave me made me think she wasn't talking about playing an instrument, but about the last time we were together. I couldn't wait until this weekend. I cleared my throat. "So, you like my hands?"

She played a few random chords, then stopped.

"I love your hands. The way you touch me, the way they feel on my body and inside me."

I wanted to break eye contact, but I couldn't. I was frozen, afraid to move. Afraid that if I blinked or breathed, this dream would vanish. It was one thing to whisper things to one another in the privacy of my bed, but out loud in public made it very real.

"Breathe, Lily." She smiled at me when I took a deep breath. She began playing a song I'd never heard.

Classical music was a gradual buildup that pulled emotions from all different corners of your heart in a slow, methodical way, but what she was playing threw me right into the thick of everything painful and loving all at once. I was stunned when she started singing. I had no idea she could sing, and so beautifully, too. Hope continued to amaze me. The words were sad. The song was about the realization of a failed relationship, and paired with the haunting music, I wanted to curl up and weep at its beauty and sorrow.

"What song is that?" It hit me how much I was missing by shutting myself off from the world and music.

"It's a song by Pink called 'But We Lost It.' A student wanted to learn it for the concert. It's simple, but so interesting to play." She played the beginning again, running over a few notes until she played it to her satisfaction.

"You sang it beautifully, too. How did I not know you sang? You continue to amaze me."

The smile on her face was one of embarrassment and pride. "We still have so much to find out about one another," she said.

Boy, did we ever. "Can you play another contemporary song for me?" I remembered the stack of sheet music she had in her apartment and knew she could pull something from memory. She started another slow song that immediately pulled me in. The notes, her voice, and the message was also sad. When she was done, we both sat in melancholy silence. "That was beautiful. I meant can you play me something that's fun and uplifting?"

She laughed. "The piano was meant for sadness. It's the best way to sulk but not be childish about it. Of course, there is fun music, and catchy songs, but I reserve the right to be sad."

I never saw the piano that way, but it made sense. I always thought the violin was the saddest instrument. "What about the other instruments? What do they tell you?"

"The harp is peaceful, never sad. The saxophone is sexy and smooth. The guitar is fun and can be sexy, too. Oh, and never underestimate the power of the trumpet. It's everything and then some," she said.

"So why isn't that your preferred instrument? I'm going to have to hear you play that, too." As a lover of jazz, I had to agree with her. The trumpet could pull out any emotion.

"I heard somebody play the piano when I was little and fell in love with it then. But I already told you that story." She stood up and walked toward me. I scooted over for her, but she sat in front of me instead. She turned her body sideways and leaned over the back of the chair to take my hands. "Hi. It's a nice surprise to see you here again."

"I missed you." I blurted that out. I tried to backpedal to calm my voice a bit. "I mean, I also missed this place. I can't even begin to explain what the Leading Note does to me."

She reached out and touched my cheek. "It's okay to miss me. And you are always welcome here anytime you want.

Now I want you to do something for me." I lifted my eyebrow at her. She reached out and squeezed my hand. "Close your eyes." I obeyed. She ran her finger across my lips, softly, as if kissing me. "Tell me what you hear."

I paused and focused. "I hear one of the instructors teaching simple chords. I always hear the traffic. A moped just drove by. There's a hum coming from the light over us. I also hear a metronome somewhere and it's driving me a little bit crazy."

Hope chuckled at that. "It's probably next door. What else do you hear?"

"The creaking of your chair." That was as far as I got before I felt Hope's full lips softly press into mine. I reached up and pulled her closer to me. She was warm and pressed her body into my touch. I snaked my hands under her shirt to feel her skin. I was desperate for her again.

"Um, we should probably be careful." She took a step back from me.

"Or we could go up to your office." I wasn't giving up. I didn't come out here for sex, but she started it with that kiss. Every part of my body was tense and tingly. I needed release.

"Or we could go up to my office." She left the room. It took me a few seconds to realize I was supposed to follow her.

When I walked out, I saw she had just reached her office door. She opened it and went in but didn't close it behind her. I casually walked up the stairs even though my heart raced ahead of me. I walked into her office. She was leaning against her desk, her legs crossed at the ankles and her ass half sitting by her in-box tray.

"Lock the door."

I obliged. "Where do you want me?" I pressed my back against the wall.

"Where do you want to be?"

I looked at the juncture of her thighs. I wanted to taste her, feel her tightness, lose myself in her wetness.

"Say it." It was almost a command. So much was happening in that moment. She wanted me to be open with her, wanted to tell me it was okay to want her and to voice what I wanted.

"I want to be between your legs." I gulped. Another big step.

Hope's mouth curved in a wicked smile. "Why are you five feet away, then?" She had a good point.

I pushed the chair out of the way, closer to the door, and stood in front of her. She reached up to cup my face and kissed me. I leaned into her and pushed everything on her desk back a foot. Things fell to the floor, but neither of us cared. I grabbed her beautiful ass and pushed her to fully sit on the edge of her desk. I slid between her now spread legs and pulled her against me. We both moaned at the intimate contact.

"Shh. You have to be quiet. We don't want anyone to hear us," I said.

"Nobody is here but a handful of employees, and they're all downstairs."

A door closed next to us and I stiffened in alarm. We waited until we heard footsteps retreat. "Liar," I whispered against her mouth.

Her lips curved in a smile. She kissed me again. "Okay, I'll be quiet."

My hands worked over the buttons of her blouse, then freed her breasts from the black bra that held them tightly together. She hissed loudly when I sucked her nipple into my mouth. I wasn't gentle.

"Shh. Quiet, love," I said.

She gulped in several deep breaths and nodded. I continued my spur-of-the-moment seduction. I loved that she was letting me lead. I reached down to unbutton her pants. They were form fitting, and I had a struggle getting them down. She leaned back on her elbows to give me better access. I was able to get her pants and panties down to mid-thigh before I gave up. I had to be inside her. I slid my fingers up and down her warm slit until I found what I wanted. I held her head close to me and plunged two fingers deep inside her. To keep from crying out, she bit down on the soft flesh between my neck and my shoulder. Her passion fueled me to fuck her harder. She leaned back again and desperately tried kicking off her shoes and pants. It wasn't working. I stopped my thrusts long enough to peel her out of her clothes until she was on the desk, naked from the waist down, breasts bared. It was the one of the most beautiful sights I'd ever seen.

"Come closer to the edge." I was impressed with how I was controlling the situation and how well she responded. She scooted until she was at the edge. The angle still wasn't great and we were both frustrated. I pulled her off the desk, kissed her hard, then turned her around. She gasped when I bent her over the desk. I had to not think and just let instinct take over. We were both too aroused to think. I spread her legs apart with mine and slipped two fingers into her. She groaned in appreciation. "Shh," I reminded her. She grabbed the front of the desk for better leverage and pushed back into my hand. I placed one hand on her bare ass to hold her down and pushed into her, slowly and as deep as I could go.

"More," she whispered hoarsely. I slipped a third finger inside her and we both moaned. She was so tight. I leaned over and nipped at her waist and the small of her back while her body grew accustomed to my third finger. "Now, Lily."

That was my cue. I pumped into her, hard, afraid I was hurting her, but her soft moans of appreciation and the fact that she begged me not to stop kept me going. Her legs stiffened and she bit down on her forearm to keep from crying out when her orgasm hit. Her whole body tensed up, her core squeezed me, and she collapsed on the desk. I was frozen in awe. I stood over her and rubbed her back while her body settled.

She started laughing quietly. "Well, I wasn't quite expecting that."

I backed away immediately. "I'm so sorry, Hope. I didn't mean…"

She rolled over and stared at me. She didn't care that she was sprawled naked in full daylight. "Are you kidding me? That was fantastic. You should come by my office more. I always knew my office had potential with you in it." She pulled up her panties and pants and sat back on the desk. I watched as she fastened her bra into place and buttoned up her shirt. "Come here." I stood between her legs again. I was slightly shaking from the intensity of the moment, afraid I did something wrong or was too rough with her. She pulled my arms around her so I was close. "That felt incredible, Lily. It was perfect. It was what I wanted, and what I needed." She kissed me until the tension left my body.

"I was worried I went too far." I touched my forehead to hers.

"I loved it. I really did." I felt a smile tug at the corner of my mouth. "I need to get back to work, but I don't want to."

We both jumped when Hope's office phone rang. She cleared her throat and answered it. "Okay, I'll be down there in a few minutes." She put her arms around me and pulled me close. "I have to go. Will I see you later?"

"Sure, if you can. I'm free." I refrained from blurting out different options. I needed to give her space and let her come to me. Today was incredible, but it also exposed my neediness. I hoped to salvage some of my integrity by giving her the option to decide if she wanted to come to my place, or wanted me at hers. I followed her out and told her to call me when she was free. She nodded, winked, and headed to her appointment. I stepped into the bathroom to clean up and straighten my clothes. I smiled at myself in the mirror. I never thought I would be somebody's girlfriend. I definitely didn't think I had it in me to go to her work, bend her over her desk, and take what I wanted while giving her the pleasure she desired.

CHAPTER TWENTY-ONE

The refrigerator was stocked. The house was clean, and I even brushed Clio and got him a little bow tie to wear. He said no in his special way that involved claws and some hissing. I gave up. He batted it around the floor until it ended up underneath the cabinet. He gave up, too. I had a television installed in my bedroom so that if we never wanted to leave the bedroom, we didn't have to. Our staycation was going to be perfect. No interruptions. I was ready to cuddle with my girlfriend for the next forty-eight hours. I expected her at nine, but she surprised me by showing up at eight fifteen.

"You're early." I pulled her inside. I kissed her soundly until she relaxed against me.

"That's okay, right?" she said as she pulled away from me to shut the door. We had a habit of making out in the doorway, much to my neighbors' surprise.

"It's wonderful." I grinned at her for no other reason than I was happy to see her.

"What?" She looked down at her outfit and then smoothed down her hair. "What's the matter?"

"Nothing. You look great. I'm just happy you're here." I grabbed her bag and set it down beside the couch. Clio was perched on the armrest, like always, to greet her.

"How is this handsome guy? Hello, big boy." She leaned down and patted his head. I rolled my eyes at his gentleness toward her. She didn't know the battle Clio and I had an hour before. She would, hopefully, find my battle scars soon.

"If you want, I can make us dinner. Or I can order from across the street. You decide. You are my guest, so whatever you're hungry for, I'll make it or order it."

"I'd rather get started on the cuddling, so how about you order Chinese and we can relax until it gets here." She sat on the couch and pulled me down next to her.

I grabbed my phone, punched in our order, and set the phone on the table. I gave her my undivided attention, as did Clio, who climbed over both of us until Hope petted him. He wasn't going to be allowed into the bedroom later, or this weekend at all.

Hope told me about her day and how the concert was pushed back a week because of both student and staff summer vacations. She said it was going to be the best one yet. Miles was going to play a song with Tyson, which was something I was looking forward to. And one of their new students was ready for a solo. The excitement was written all over her face.

"Do you ever go on vacation, or is the Leading Note everything to you?" I was curious when her last real break was. I was even more curious to find out who it was with.

"Really, I love it so much it doesn't feel like work." She held my hand and rubbed my palm with her thumb.

"When was your last vacation?"

"I went to Vermont with my ex-girlfriend about four years ago." She shrugged apologetically.

I found that it stung just a little bit even though it was a long time ago. "That sounds nice." I gritted my teeth and kept a small smile plastered in place. This was jealousy. I couldn't help but wonder if she and her girlfriend did the same things we did.

"What about you? When was your last vacation?"

I snorted. My last vacation was twelve years ago when my grandparents took me to Florida to play on the beach. I hated the sun, I hated the sand, and I hated that everyone in my life was trying to force me to be a normal teenager. I'd just gone through a major meltdown, and nobody cared. Well, my parents did, only because it forced them to focus their attention elsewhere like getting jobs and their own lives. My grandparents thought I could just stand up, dust myself off, and be okay. After that disastrous trip, they decided I needed more therapy. "A long time ago. I went to Florida with my grandparents. It was okay."

"You didn't take any trips in college? No wild and crazy spring breaks?" She bumped her shoulder against me, forcing me to put my arm around her. She snuggled up close.

"No. I pretty much went to school full-time. Even on breaks I worked on projects. I didn't have any friends in college, not that I would have gone anywhere with them." I wasn't sad. It was just a matter of fact.

"My college was kind of crazy. I worked a lot, but I did have tons of friends. I'm sorry you didn't. You are such a nice person." She squeezed my hand.

"Thank you, but I didn't really miss out. If I'd met people like you and your friends in college, maybe I would have been more interested in a social life." I kissed the back of her hand. The intercom buzzed, signaling dinner had arrived. I'd ordered us large portions of orange chicken, fried rice, and lo mein with pork because I knew we'd nibble on it later. "Oh, I forgot to tell you. I have a surprise for you back in the bedroom."

Hope lifted her eyebrow at me and smirked. "Tell me it's something fun to try in bed."

I blushed and stammered nonsensical words. "Um, no. Nothing like that, but something else. I can show you after dinner." I looked down at my plate. I wanted to slip under the table and disappear.

"You're adorable, Lily. So innocent, yet only about certain things." She looked at me and winked.

I blushed harder. I thought about Wednesday in her office and bending her over the desk. That was so unlike anything I could ever imagine, but now that it had happened, I couldn't stop visualizing us in different positions, in different rooms, in public places. I was obsessing about it. I'd let my instincts take over the other day with her and was handsomely rewarded. I decided to follow my instincts again.

"Wednesday was nice," I said like it was a walk in the park. I took a bite of orange chicken and chewed, not breaking eye contact with Hope.

"You called me love in my office," she said.

I choked on that piece of chicken and jumped up from the table. I did what? Hope raced over to my side. She patted my back as I coughed to dislodge the food that was stuck in my throat. Little did she know my heart and stomach were there, too. I replayed the scene. I sure as fuck did call her love.

I waved her off as if her smacks weren't helping, but I really just needed a moment to calm down and let everything settle. I walked to the window and looked out while my stomach returned to its rightful place. My heart wasn't budging, though. Hope handed me a glass a water and I drank it in ten seconds. I took a deep breath and turned to her.

"I said what?"

"It was a caught-up-in-the-moment kind of thing. Don't worry about it." She stood beside me and rubbed my back.

It was soothing, but I was so on edge from what she said that I couldn't appreciate it. I took a step away from her. A flash of disappointment crossed her face, but she nodded at me and retreated back to the table. I was such an insensitive jerk. This could have been my moment. The moment when I told Hope that I loved her and maybe she would say it back to me, but no, I had to brush her off like her comfort wasn't appreciated. The special moment was gone no matter what I did to try to salvage it. I walked back over to the table.

"I'm sorry. You caught me off guard."

"Are you okay?" She seemed genuinely concerned.

"Yeah, that was a tough swallow." I cowardly decided to ignore what she said and grasped at anything else to discuss. "So, I tried to dress Clio up for you tonight, but he wouldn't cooperate." Lame. "I'll show you the battle scars later." I was so bad at this.

"Dress up how?" At least she played along.

"I got him this super cute yellow and blue bow tie, but he thought I was trying to choke him and put up quite the fight. He shoved it under the cabinet somewhere." I pushed my plate away from me. My appetite was gone. "Look. I'm sorry I'm bad at girlfriend stuff." I held my hand up when she began protesting. "I'm learning and I know I'm not easy, but I really am trying. My social skills and how I communicate are awful. I know this, but please know that I'm trying."

Hope stood and came over to me. She knelt in front of me and took my hands in hers. "Listen to me. I knew going in that you're shy and you don't have a lot of experience hanging around people. I'm glad you're not silver-tongued and can just spew out the perfect thing to say. As bad as this is to say, it's actually kind of fun to see how you react in certain situations. I shouldn't have sprung what you said Wednesday on you. That wasn't fair. The time will come and then we can joke about this." She cupped my chin and kissed me softly.

"You are too good to me, Hope."

"Are you done eating for now? We can box this up and try again in about an hour when we're both hungry again. You know what they say about Chinese food."

I smiled. She shooed me away to the couch and cleaned up. I sat and closed my eyes. Clio jumped on the couch and curled up on my lap. Even though he favored Hope, he always knew when I was having one of my meltdown moments. He calmed me. By the time Hope joined us, my heart rate was back to normal and I could look her in the eye.

"Thank you."

"It's no problem. Tell me about this surprise you have for me." She sat on the couch next to me.

"Wait. It's a surprise I have to show you." I motioned for her to get up.

She groaned. "Really? You couldn't have said this before I got comfy?"

I stood and pulled her up. "It's really not that big a deal." I grabbed her bag with my free hand and playfully pulled her into my bedroom.

Her eyes locked on the television. "Oh, this is nice, Lily. We'll never leave this room. Ever."

Hope always said the right thing.

"Go put your pajamas on and I'll find us something to watch." I found the remotes for the television and the sound system. I removed some of the pillows from the bed, put Clio outside the door and closed it, and crawled under the covers.

"Honestly, I didn't pack pajamas, so I hope this works," Hope said.

I looked at her and my jaw almost hit the floor. She was wearing black panties and a black lacy camisole. Hope D'Marco was stunning in black. Whatever movie I found for us to watch was forgotten the second my hands touched her body.

❖

"Are you sure you have to leave in an hour?" I playfully whined.

Hope was tucked in the crook of my arm and we'd just finished breakfast in bed with one another for dessert. It was almost noon on Sunday, time for her to get up, get ready, and spend some time with her family. It was their weekend ritual and I didn't want to interrupt it. She invited me along, but I quickly declined.

"Come shower with me. We've been in bed so long, I think I've forgotten how to move." She dragged me from the bed.

"Oh, I think you moved just fine all weekend long." My mind flashed back to all the different positions we tried, liked, and repeated over and over again. I was sore everywhere, but I wasn't going to let it slow me down. I wasn't even going to let Hope know my body was tested.

"Come on. We'll conserve water." She winked at me and tugged my hand until I caved and got off the bed.

"Remember what happened the last time we conserved water?"

She answered by kissing my neck, gently biting the soft skin.

I shivered. "I guess you do remember."

"How could I forget? You were so delicious pressed against the back of the shower."

I shuddered again. Last night, Hope turned me and bent me over slightly so she could taste me at a different angle.

It was so decadent and I felt so wanton that I came within just a few minutes. I'd had eight orgasms that weekend, and number nine was going to happen soon. She pulled me under the stream of hot water and ran her hands over my body to ensure every part of me got wet. She ran her fingers up and down my slit, then slipped between the swollen folds. I moaned my appreciation.

"Remember, you're the one on a schedule," I said.

"Remember, you're the one who can come in thirty seconds."

"Checkmate." I spread my legs to give her better access and leaned back so the water sprayed over my hair and down my back. Every part of me felt fantastic. Hope was right. It took less than a minute to feel the first quivers of my orgasm. She slipped a finger inside me and continued to rub her thumb on my clit. I grabbed her shoulders and pulled her to me when I came.

"I can't tell if I'm jealous or if I'm the best lover in the world because you come so hard and so fast." She slipped out of me.

"Best lover in the world. Best lover to me." We both smiled, knowing she had been my only lover. I whined again when she turned off the water. "Are we done here?"

"In the shower? Yes. I can't have orgasms standing, and I definitely want another before I have to leave. Let's go back to bed."

She handed me a towel and I quickly dried off.

I knew we were pressed for time, but I needed to taste her because I wouldn't again until next weekend. The concert was Friday, so Hope would be busy with extra practices all week. I crawled on top of her slowly, touching her everywhere. She grabbed my towel, opened it, and pulled me into her. For the next twenty minutes, we communicated, but not with words. I missed her warmth when she left the bed to get ready.

"Are you sure you don't want to join me?" She leaned back to look at me from the vanity. She held her mascara brush in one hand and dabbed her finger on her bottom lip to smooth out her lipstick with the other. Her hair was pulled back in a long ponytail. I took my time appreciating her form. She rolled her eyes at me. "So, I guess that's a no."

"One day I might. Baby steps, okay?" I pulled my T-shirt over my head. I wanted to at least walk her to the door.

"Have you seen my phone?" Hope picked her towel up from the chair and shook it. She made her way around the room, lifting pillows and piles of clothes we'd discarded.

I joined in but gave up the search after about ten seconds. I picked up my phone and dialed her number.

"What are you doing?"

"I'm calling you. Your phone has to be here somewhere. We'll hear it." I smiled at her.

"No, Lily. Don't."

It was too late. From underneath my pillow came the chords of "Stars at Twilight in A Flat Major." It was slow and hauntingly beautiful. I'd forgotten how easily it stirred up my emotions. I knew the song by heart. I knew it because I wrote it and the recording was me playing it. Her ringtone for me was my own music. Well, Jillian Crest's music. She stopped moving and stared at me, her eyes large with fear.

Another shift was taking place inside me, but this time, I was back onstage, and all the broken pieces I had painfully put back together over the years shattered. The blood rushed from my head and I was overcome with a cold so frightening I had to sit down.

"You've known this whole time," I said.

"Lily, wait. Let me explain." She fell to her knees in front of me.

I felt myself shutting down from the inside out. My heart, a glacier chunk of hard ice, stopped beating when I looked into her eyes. I was alone. She was no longer a part of me.

"Get out."

CHAPTER TWENTY-TWO

I ignored my phone the rest of the day. I couldn't bear to stay in the bedroom, so I grabbed a pillow and a blanket and headed for the couch. I couldn't focus on anything, but I had to do something to try to keep my mind off Hope. I turned on a mindless sci-fi movie that didn't keep my interest, but it was loud and helped drown out my broken thoughts. Hope knew I was Jillian Crest. Looking back over the last few months, I noticed tiny signs. At the museum, she got between me and the man who recognized me from my youth. She never questioned me about my education or why I knew so much about music. Nobody did that. No musician would accept help from someone without knowing their musical background.

Clio recognized my foul mood and did his best to snap me out of it, but this was beyond a simple snuggle fix. I was destroyed. I cried for four hours straight. I cried myself to sleep and when I woke up, contorted on the couch, I cried some more. I dragged myself to the bathroom and took a long, hot shower. It was Monday morning and I just couldn't work. I called in sick for the first time ever. The day was a blur. I faded in and out of restless sleep. I tried to eat but could only pick at food. Tuesday wasn't any better. I even skipped therapy. I didn't feel like talking about this ever.

Wednesday was the turning point. I had one of my horrific nightmares. For the first time ever, my nightmare wasn't about performing. It was about Hope. Images of her flashed in my nightmare. I was in a deep, dark cave and was reaching up to the light. Hope's face peered over the side, and instead of helping me, she laughed at me. I woke up sweating and shaking. That got me off the couch. I needed to shower and at least get back to work. I slipped into a pair of jeans and a T-shirt and put my hair up in a bun.

I made a cup of tea while I reviewed my email. Shit. I forgot about picking up the check on Monday. My banker sent me an email reminding me about it, then a follow-up asking if I wanted to reinvest it instead. No, I wanted to help out the organization, and this was my way. With any luck, I could get in, slip it to Agnes, and get out. I knew that Jeremy would gladly handle the transaction, but I was a glutton for punishment. I had to do it. I was pissed and sad and felt betrayed. The old me would have accepted Jeremy's help, but the new me needed to prove a point. Before, I was frightened and hid from the world. I still wanted to hide, but only from Hope. I wasn't likely to see her, so I needed to go for it. I wrote Jeremy and told him I'd be there before lunch. I still wanted it to be anonymous, but in a petty way, I also wanted Hope to know about my donation. I wanted her to feel bad. Completely childish, but it was the first real emotion I'd felt besides anger in almost three days.

"Give me strength," I said to Clio on my way out.

I slipped on my sunglasses and headed to the train. It was after the morning commute, so the train wasn't packed. I found a seat and got comfortable. I kept my sunglasses on and looked out the window. I now understood what having a broken heart meant. Reading about it or watching it on the big screens was one thing; experiencing it was soul crushing. I was already broken before I met Hope. She built me up, patched up the cracks, then smashed me in completely new ways. I'd trusted her more than anyone else in this world. I knew she had tried to reach out to me several times. My cell phone rang several times and dinged with text messages until I finally turned it off. It was still at home. I just didn't have the energy to bring it with me.

By the time I got to the bank, I was a mess. I stood outside until the tears stopped. Several people looked at me as they walked by. I waved off the ones who stopped to ask if I was okay. I could do this. I could go in there and get the check. The problem was after I had the check in my hands. Could I really go to the Leading Note? Could I risk running into Hope? The anger bubbled up again. I knew that I would need answers, but it would be a long time before I could face her.

"Lily, I was beginning to wonder if you were going to show up or not. It's good to see you." Jeremy walked toward me and shook my hand. He was always nice to me. Maybe that was because I had a lot of money invested in his bank, but I was willing to give him the benefit of the doubt.

"I'm sorry for the delay. I've been under the weather lately." I sat down across from him.

"How are things? Ready to dip into your savings and take a vacation somewhere tropical? Or maybe somewhere cold? This heat has been relentless." He unlocked his desk and handed me an envelope with a cashier's check.

"Not this time." I didn't feel like chitchatting with a stranger. It was remarkable that I even sat down. In the past, I would have grabbed the check and bolted.

"Any other business you'd like to discuss? We have several investment options," he said. And I was done. There was no way I could talk about money today. I stood up, thanked him for his time, and left. Hour by hour, I was slipping back into the old Lily, the one who wanted to stay hidden from the world.

❖

"It's always nice to see you," Agnes said to me as she climbed the steps to the front door. "It's too hot to be outside. Come on in. Hope isn't here right now, but if you want to wait for her, she'll be back in about thirty minutes."

I jumped up with relief and followed her inside. "I'm not here for Hope. I'm actually here for you."

"Oh? Well, then let's head up to my office. Do you want a glass of water or something to drink?"

"No, thank you. I don't have a lot of time. I just wanted to drop this off." I handed her the envelope.

"What's this?" She opened it and turned the check over several times. She stared at me in disbelief.

"I know you lost some local funding recently, and I just wanted to help out," I said.

She clutched me to her and hugged me tightly. "This is wonderful, Lily. I can't wait to share the news. Does Hope know?"

"No, and I hate to say this, but I don't want Hope to know. I just want this to be between us."

"But this will help us out so much. I think Hope should know." She stared at the check again. "I don't mean to pry, but did something happen with you two? She seems so sad lately, and you were a little too relieved when I mentioned she wasn't going to be here for a bit."

Fuck. I could feel the tears start. I looked down at the worn chair and played with a piece of string that had unraveled from the bronze upholstery tack. I needed to get out of there.

"I should go. Thanks, Agnes, for taking care of this."

She hugged me again, this time a little bit longer than necessary. "You take care of yourself, Lily. And thank you again."

I left in a hurry and didn't allow the tears to fall until I cleared the stairs outside. How could I cry so much in such a short time? I headed for the station, anxious to get back home and safe where I belonged. Just me and Clio, like we were before, like we should have always been.

CHAPTER TWENTY-THREE

I still don't feel the greatest, so I'm going to work from home." I threw in a tiny cough for good measure even though I didn't have to. My voice was scratchy and I sounded nasal from crying so much.

"Just take care of yourself, don't worry about anything. We'll handle things." My boss seemed like he wasn't sure how to handle me since I never called in sick or wanted vacation time.

"Thanks. I'll see you next week." I hung up before he continued to talk. I would have confessed after a few more seconds because I was a horrible liar. The big concert was that night. The thing I was looking forward to the most, but I couldn't let myself go. I still hadn't listened to any voice mails or read any text messages. I knew the moment I did, my life would be thrust right back into the hell from last Sunday. I wasn't ready. I puttered around on the internet for a few minutes but closed it when everything I saw reminded me of Hope. I wanted to hole up, but I felt cooped up. I walked around like a caged animal until Clio started following me. I needed to go somewhere, but I wasn't sure where. Maybe I could head north for the weekend. Take a train somewhere. Hit the water. Clio would be okay for two days without me.

I found a trip that was a three-hour train ride, but then I remembered I would be stuck on a train with people I didn't know for three hours. I could barely handle the L and knew I could jump off at any station if it got too overwhelming. I plopped down on the couch and sighed. I was stuck here. Maybe I could go for a walk. I checked the temperature. It was already hot and my energy level was low. I jumped in the shower and got ready, hoping something would spark my interest. Maybe there was a nice exhibit at one of the museums. I braided back my hair, pinched my cheeks to get color and circulation back in them, and grabbed my purse.

"Good-bye, my love." I rubbed Clio's torn ear affectionately. He was probably glad I was getting out of the house. He was so concerned because of my breakdown, I don't think he slept the twenty hours a day he normally got.

I opened the door and gasped. Hope stood in my doorway, her arm up as if to knock. My eyes narrowed quickly. My pulse quickened and the blood that I just had to pinch up to my cheeks, now flooded them.

"What are you doing here?" I asked.

"I really want us to talk." She looked tired and sad. The dark circles under her eyes rivaled mine, and I gained a little bit of satisfaction knowing that she was miserable, too.

"I really don't think we have anything to say to one another." That was a lie. I had a million things to say to her, but I think she already knew most of them. "How did you get up here?" This building was secure. Nobody made exceptions.

"Can I just come in for a minute, just one minute, and talk? I hope you at least can forgive me long enough for me to explain things."

Fuck. She looked so sad and vulnerable, but damn it, she should be. I couldn't imagine a scenario where this was okay, where lying to me was perfectly acceptable. I had lied, too, but my lie was self-preservation and a decision I made years ago. I stood in front of her, my hands clenched in fists, and stared at her. She reached out and gently put her hands on my wrists. I jerked at her touch but didn't pull away.

"Please? Just a minute. Then I'll leave and you'll never hear from me again."

I gave a half nod and stepped back. She walked in, ignored Clio, and asked me to have a seat on the couch.

"A long time ago, you asked me how I got into music. Do you remember that?" She wanted me to answer.

"Yes."

"I told you that my mom took me to the symphony, but I never told you anything about it. I saw you, young Jillian Crest, at the piano and I was completely stunned. I was eleven, you were eight, and you had mastered everything you played. I was in awe of you. I begged my mom to give me piano lessons for my birthday. I promised her I would stick with them all because of you." Hope began pacing the same path I had earlier that morning. She stopped and turned to me. "I followed your career for years until you just ceased to exist. Nobody knew what happened to you. You just disappeared."

I shrugged my shoulders and tried to look unaffected by Hope's confession. That was one scenario I hadn't considered. "That was when I had my breakdown. The first of many, I suppose." My answer was more of a whisper, but she heard me.

She dropped to her knees in front of me. "You gave me a love for the piano. Your symphonies made me branch out to different instruments. Then, when I saw you again at the concert at our little center, my heart stopped. I had to play it cool because I thought it was you, but I wasn't sure. When Agnes saw you at Bleachers and told me your name, I was crushed. I thought for sure you were Jillian." She took a deep breath and held my hands. "But then we talked and I knew just by your musical advice that you were Jillian. I felt it. I knew it was you. Plus, you look the same, really, only older."

I stood to put space between us. She was getting through to me and I needed to put up more of a fight. I needed answers.

"Why didn't you say anything to me then?" I would have freaked out if she said my old name and we both knew it.

She gave me a small smile. "You would have bolted out of the door never to be seen again. I know you don't see it, but I was respecting your wishes for your privacy. The more I got to know you, the more I realized how private you were."

"So, you were being kind to me." I sneered.

"Stop. Put yourself in my place. You wanted everyone to forget about you. You dropped out of sight, changed your name, and started doing something completely different with your life. Who was I to bring it up? I was respecting your choices. I knew that, in time, you would tell me." She leaned away from me and hung her head.

I hated that she was right. Everything she said was spot-on, but that didn't mean I didn't feel betrayed. I leaned back on the couch, utterly exhausted already. Relationships were hard. Love was fantastic, but when you hit the ceiling, the force of the fall left you breathless.

"I never wanted to be Jillian again," I whispered. A tear pushed through my wall. Another one fell, and another. I was angry at myself for crying, for being weak in front of Hope.

"Lily, I don't know what happened to you or why it happened, but what I did was truly out of respect. I was waiting for you to come to me. I knew you would eventually. Who was I to push you?"

"You're my girlfriend. Or were my girlfriend."

"Don't say that. Please don't say that," she said. She wiped a tear away. "We will get through this." She stood and leaned over me. "We will, Lily. I'm not giving up on us and I won't let you either."

I slid away from her. "You can't even begin to understand what happened to me. I don't really know it myself." I gave a bitter snort of a laugh. "Music turned on me. It was once in my blood, but then it became a poison. Everyone in my life expected me to be the best all the time. I used to pretend to be asleep so that I didn't have to play every waking minute of my life." The tension and energy of my past pushed me up and I started pacing again.

Hope stood in my path and reached for my hands. "There is still beautiful music inside you. I can tell. If you want to find it again, you will."

I shook free from her. She'd said a lot of very powerful things to me today. My thoughts were loud and I needed to process and quiet them.

"Look, Hope, I appreciate that you stopped by to explain things to me."

"I never meant to hurt you. I only wanted to love you," she said.

I closed my eyes. She did not just say that to me.

"Please go."

She turned, gave Clio a quick scratch, and headed for the door. "I hope you can forgive me. I miss you. I miss us." She gave me a quick, sad smile and walked out.

It took only five seconds for me to collapse on the couch into another sobbing mess.

CHAPTER TWENTY-FOUR

D
r. Monroe sat across from me and smiled at me for the first time in a long time. "Your breakthrough is quite remarkable. It's been a long time coming."

"Couldn't you have warned me that it was going to be exhausting? I haven't slept or cried this much in years."

"How do you feel, though? Are you happy you and Hope talked?"

"I don't know that I would call it happy. What she said made sense, but I'm having a hard time forgiving her. I haven't trusted people in a very long time, so I don't know how to let go." I sat in silence and thought about the last week of my life. After Sunday, I was just going to go back to my solitary life and forget Hope even happened, but then she had to show up unannounced and make me reconsider. I had to decide if I wanted to accept her apology and her explanation. She made my heart flutter even though I was upset with her. Around her, I heard life differently.

"Our time's up, but I want you to think about all the good that's come from your relationship with Hope. Keep that in mind." Dr. Monroe walked me out when our session was over.

She was right. Life was better with Hope in it, but how could I let go? How could I stop being so stubborn? I was so good at self-sabotage. I'd missed the concert, and even though Hope told me she was going to leave it up to me to contact her, I checked my phone. A lot. My heart sank further when it showed an empty screen. I wanted her to text me. I didn't know how to reach out to her. I was skittish by nature and a complete bumbling idiot with words, especially the apologetic kind.

I grabbed an early dinner from down the street on my way home, and Clio and I did what I do best: sulked. I turned on a marathon of a zombie show, grabbed some chopsticks, and curled up on the couch again. When my phone rang, I jumped. It was Agnes. I panicked. Something was wrong. Something was wrong with Hope. I answered immediately.

"Hello?"

"Lily? Hi, it's Agnes. How are you?"

I forced myself to relax. Agnes would have told me right away if she was calling because something was wrong. Besides, why would she even tell me?

"I'm okay. What's going on?"

"I wanted to thank you and tell you the good news if you don't already know. You probably already do, but Banks Corporation gave us a five-year lease on a building they aren't using. It's closer to our old location and it's just perfect. I know you are behind this. We're going to use your money to help renovate and soundproof the rooms and maybe even get newer furniture. I'm just so happy you found us, Lily. Thank you so much."

I was stunned. I knew that my company would want to help out, but that was way above and beyond what I expected. I thought maybe they'd donate a few thousand dollars, but this? This generosity floored me.

"That's great, Agnes. That even surprises me. When did you find out?"

"About two minutes ago. I'm just in shock."

I wanted to ask if Hope knew. Excitement bubbled up inside me, pushing aside my anger and my stubbornness. I was going to have to call my boss as soon as I got off the phone with Agnes.

"I can't wait to tell the others. I wanted to call and thank you first, though."

My mind was already two steps ahead. Their lease was up in a few months. What about the new kids they acquired from that neighborhood? Would they continue their lessons in the new place? How were they going to move everything? The baby grand was going to be a bitch to move. And those instruments? Some of them needed to be recycled. Correction. They needed to be retired.

"Sure, sure, Agnes. You're welcome. I think Leading Note does amazing work and I'm happy to be a part of it."

I called Gene the second we hung up. "You gave them the Bennington building? That's incredible." I sounded happy even to myself.

"We don't have any plans for it anytime soon, and this is a great way to help out. This is the first thing you've ever been excited about, and you're one of our best employees. Plus, my daughter-in-law wants to do a story on it when they get set up. It will be good for us and for them."

I couldn't argue that logic. Any exposure for Leading Note would be appreciated, even if it was more for Banks' benefit. Gene's daughter-in-law worked as a feature reporter for WGN. She was cute and popular and had a large following.

"Thank you. That was incredibly thoughtful." I loved my company even more right now. I was excited for Leading Note. This was the best case scenario for them, and I was proud to be a part of it.

I hung up with Gene and grabbed my laptop to study the

location. It was close to the place where they were before, so Hope was probably pumped. My money was a chunk, but I doubted it would go far with the costs it would take to convert the building and soundproof the walls. I told myself to relax. This wasn't my problem. I kept telling myself that as I grabbed my purse and walked out the door. I even forgot to say good-bye to Clio.

CHAPTER TWENTY-FIVE

I walked right up the steps and into the Leading Note. Nobody was at the front desk, and all of the music rooms were either occupied or locked. I went up the steps to the second level and pretended I was just waiting for Hope to suddenly appear, but I had a mission. I needed to talk to Hope. I opened the door to the concert room and closed it behind me.

I took a deep breath and walked the twenty steps to the Steinway baby grand. I circled it, admired the soundboard, and ran my fingers along the smooth edge of the piano. I was familiarizing myself with it. I wondered if we'd connect well. I pulled out the bench at just the right distance, wiggled down on it until I was comfortable, and lifted the fallboard. My heart leapt and fluttered in my throat. I placed my hands on the keys and waited to see if I was going to freak out, but all I felt was excitement. The good kind that made me want to press down on the keys. I hit four successive notes. A flat, C, E flat, and A flat. The keys were touch sensitive and adjusted for children's hands, which made me smile. I momentarily forgot I was at a center that specifically taught children. The keys returned to my hand effortlessly. I was used to this setup. I brushed my fingertips along the tops of the keys, barely touching them, pressing them just to get a feel but not to make a sound. It was time and I was ready.

I played "The Entertainer" by Scott Joplin as my quick warm-up before I dug into one of my own songs. "Stars at Twilight in A Flat Major" had been on my mind since I heard it on Hope's phone. I eased into it. The entire piece was just under sixteen minutes. It was ambitious for my first time back in over a decade, but the need to play it again was strong. Hope was the first person to get me to listen to classical music again and the first one who made me want to play it in over a decade.

The first movement was shorter than most pieces, but I'd wanted to get the interest of the listener immediately instead of lulling them into the song. It was a battle with one of my mentors, but I won because I was good—no, I was great at eliciting emotions right away with my music. The one thing that made me stand out from all of the other child prodigies I'd known was that I felt the music from a place I couldn't explain. It was deeper than in my soul. When I lost that focus and made it my mission to conquer everything and everyone, I lost that connection. I fell apart once I realized music was greater than anything I could comprehend and I was merely its outlet.

Once I hit the third movement, I found a change that I wanted to make. I would note it when I was done. I didn't want to interrupt the flow since it had taken so long to get to this point. This piano was lovely, a classic that Hope obviously took care of. I had been afraid it wouldn't be in tune or I would have to adjust my playing to the weight of the keys, but it was almost perfect. By the time I was done, I was exhausted. Emotionally drained. I closed the fallboard, leaned forward so that my elbows rested on it, and cried. I was so tired of crying, but these tears were liberating. All of the therapy to get me to this point, all of the love I finally felt for people and things, came down to this moment.

"Lily, oh, my God. That was…"

I turned in alarm. Hope was leaning against the wall, tears that matched mine streaming down her cheeks. I wasn't ready for her to be here. I wasn't ready to face her while feeling this vulnerable.

"You weren't supposed to be here," I said quietly.

"I'm so happy that I was. That was beautiful, Lily. Incredible." She walked toward me, brushing the tears off her cheeks. I couldn't look at her yet. She was respectful of my wishes and kept her distance, finally sitting in a chair in the front row.

I was here for a reason. Playing her piano was a whim—a life changing one, but I was there to talk to Hope. I finally looked at her. She bit her bottom lip to keep from crying again. I hated to see her cry. Even though I was guarded, seeing tears on her cheeks was heartbreaking. We were both crying for the same reason, but I was still responsible and it hurt to see someone I loved cry.

"I came here because you were right." I held up my hand when she stood to walk over to me. She sat back down and waited for me to finish. "I did change my name and walked away from music. I figured if I stayed away from music, it would return the favor. Instead, I heard you play, and that sparked something inside me again, but I had to do it in my own way. Even though you respected my wishes and I get why you didn't tell me, it still hurt." I stood up and walked away. I wasn't leaving, I just needed to put more space between us. Communicating wasn't my strongest suit, so I had to think before I blurted out the wrong thing. "I didn't plan for this to happen. Us. I didn't know how I was going to tell you or anyone about the old me. I didn't realize how important it was until our friendship took a turn. Then I got scared."

"Lily, I really didn't mean to hurt you or lie to you. That's not who I am. I want us to work. I want to be with you, Lily Croft. I thought I was doing the right thing by waiting for you to tell me, but maybe I should have dropped hints or said something sooner. I just knew you were scared and that this was a big step for you. You literally fell off the face of the earth thirteen years ago." She stood but didn't approach me. "You were so important to me then and even more so now, but in a totally new way." She was going to cry again, which meant I was going to cry, too.

"I want us to work, too. Can we start over?" I asked.

"No."

I looked at her in surprise. "No?"

"No. We can take a few steps back, but I don't want to start over. Getting through to you is my biggest accomplishment. I want you. I want to hold your hand and watch movies. I want to kiss you again. I miss your lips and your tenderness. I even miss Clio and his sweet face." She walked over to me. I stood firm. "I need you in my life as my girlfriend. Yes, we can slow down until you can trust me again, but no, I'm not starting over."

I almost smiled at the fierceness I saw in her eyes. She was serious, and I felt my heart flutter up and threaten to jump out of my chest at her devotion. Hope was everything I ever wanted. "Okay. I can do that."

"Will you have dinner with me tonight? Or sometime soon?"

"Today is kind of overwhelming. Can we try for tomorrow?"

She smiled and nodded. "I can bring food over and maybe

we can talk more about this." She paused at my reaction. "Or we can just move past this and talk when you are ready."

"Okay." I stood there awkwardly because even though I didn't want to leave, I really needed time to myself.

She reached out and squeezed my hand. "I'll see you tomorrow about six thirty. Thank you for giving me another chance."

I walked out of the building even though I wanted to run. These goddamn tears were going to be the death of me.

Chapter Twenty-six

I took the day off. I deserved it. When I got home yesterday after talking to Hope, I could barely sit still. I was exhausted but couldn't sleep. I had played the piano. For the first time in thirteen years, I wasn't afraid of it. I wanted to call Dr. Monroe, but it was well after hours, so I sent her an email telling her about my day instead. She knew I was on the cusp of another breakthrough but wanted me to find out for myself. We were going to have a lot to talk about later this week.

"Are you excited that you get to see Hope again? I know I am." Clio was in the windowsill, but instead of being interested in the world outside, he was watching me pace. It was ridiculous, so I sat on the couch. He sauntered to me and curled up on my lap. There was nothing for me to do but watch the clock. I'd cleaned the condo all morning, picked up snacks at the market downstairs, and taken the longest, hottest shower until the water cooled. I was going to change before Hope came over. My clothes were already out and ready to slip into. When my phone rang, I panicked. It was Hope.

"Hello?" I was so afraid she was going to cancel.

"Hi. I know it's early, but my schedule freed up and I was wondering if I could come over early. As long as that doesn't mess you up."

I closed my eyes and counted to five before I answered. My schedule was completely out of whack, and I had to learn to adjust or I would fall back into the hole it took so long to climb out of. Plus, I was happy. "What time are you thinking, because Clio and I are on the couch doing absolutely nothing but waiting for you."

"I've missed your quiet humor," she said. It made me smile. "I was thinking about thirty minutes? Is that okay?"

I couldn't get Clio off my lap fast enough. My heart pounded as I rushed to my room to get dressed.

"That's fine." I sounded winded even to myself. I held the phone away from my mouth and took a deep breath. "We'll be here."

I hung up and I stripped off what I was wearing and slipped on the new dress that was spread out on my bed. It was bright and yellow with thin straps. Even though we were taking things slow, I wanted to look nice. I carefully applied makeup, just enough to look natural. I pulled my hair back with a tie but left it long down the center of my back. Hope once told me she loved my hair down, even though I thought it was wild. The intercom buzzed and set me in a tailspin. Had thirty minutes already passed? I took three deep breaths before I answered it. She was here. Clio was perched on the arm of the couch, almost as if he knew Hope was coming over.

"Hi," Hope said. I melted at how beautiful she looked. She wore a red summer dress that ended below her knees but hugged her curves nicely. Her hair was down and rested over her shoulder. I almost pulled her into my arms, but I remembered we weren't there yet. "Can I come in?"

I immediately stood back and allowed her entry. I'd already forgotten my manners. "Sorry about that."

"Hi, Clio. Did you miss me?" She rubbed the top of his head and scratched his chin when he lifted his face to her for easier access. "I got you something." She reached into her purse and pulled out a fresh sprig of catnip. He turned wild immediately and batted it out of her hand. Hope wisely dropped it.

"I'm sorry, but did you just give my cat drugs?"

"He's never had catnip before?"

We watched as he rubbed over the sprig, bit it, shook it, and flung it across the room only to chase immediately after it.

"Huh. I guess not. I don't know how I feel about him having it. Hopefully, you didn't get him hooked on a bad habit."

"My mom's cat loves it and she's still sweet. When it's not around," she said. "Maybe that was a bad idea." She pointed to Clio, who was now hiding under a dining room chair with the catnip tucked underneath him. She turned to me after ten seconds of staring at my weird cat. "Are you hungry?"

"I think so." I was too nervous to eat, but I went through the motions. I stood beside her while we fixed our plates. Shrimp stir-fry and veggie rolls. She didn't give me a hard time when I only put a little bit on my plate. I grabbed a bottle of wine, Hope's favorite chardonnay, and joined her at the dining room table.

"How was work?" she asked.

"I took the day off."

"Wow. You never take time off. Good for you."

"Yesterday was a big day for me, and I knew I wasn't going to be able to concentrate today, so Clio and I hung out instead." She didn't need to know that I'd cleaned my place from top to bottom, done eight loads of neglected laundry, and taken a nap since sleep was fleeting last night.

"Can we talk about yesterday?"

I took a deep breath and nodded. "Yesterday was big."

"Yesterday was huge." She reached over and squeezed

my forearm. "I don't know if this means anything to you, but I'm very proud of you."

"Thank you. I don't know if I meant to play, but I went there to find you and my journey took a turn. I stopped on the second floor instead of heading up to your office. I saw the piano and just went for it. It's a beautiful piano. You take such good care of it." I took a small bite of food so I wouldn't choke on it, and washed it down with a large mouthful of wine.

"I literally hung up on the person I was talking to because I could hear it and I wondered who was playing your music as well as you do. The thought that it was you didn't even cross my mind." She touched my hand briefly. "I'm sorry I sneaked in, but I couldn't help myself. I wanted to burst open at everything I was feeling. I was happy, and proud, and overwhelmed. It was so incredible."

I offered her a small smile. I was proud of myself, too, but playing made me vulnerable again. "I didn't think I would remember it after so long, but it flowed well, I thought." I shrugged like it was no big deal.

"See? Here's the part where I'm trying not to fangirl over you and I'm just pretending I'm having dinner with my girlfriend who definitely isn't one of the best pianists and composers of our time. Just dinner. Just hanging out."

Hope was good for my ego, especially my old one. Maybe I did still have it, but I refused to let it consume me like it did before. "You're sweet. Thank you for everything you've done for me to get me to this point."

She leaned over and kissed my cheek. Her warm breath against my skin made me shiver. It was impossible for me not to have a reaction around her. I knew what her mouth, her hands, her body was capable of. Love, appreciation, and devotion.

"Thank you for letting me into your life and giving me a second chance."

Too wound up to eat, I pushed my plate away but kept my wineglass in front of me. Since meeting Hope, I found I enjoyed wine, especially the calmness that washed over me after a glass. I needed to relax tonight.

"This is a second chance, right?" she asked.

"Yes." I didn't know what else to say.

"Thank you." She quickly brushed away a tear.

I pretended that I didn't see it. I didn't want this night to turn into a pile of mush. I wanted to stay strong and ride this confident high for as long as I could. We cleaned up and headed to the couch.

"Where do you think Clio is?" I couldn't find him in the living room or the dining room.

"He probably packed a bag and is headed to Catnipville. I'm afraid I created a monster." We heard a growl and a scuffle down the hall.

"Way to go," I said.

She leaned against me and I automatically put my arm around her. "Can we talk about us? Or can I tell you how I feel and what I want?"

I looked at her in surprise.

"Not that I'm making demands here. Please don't think that. I just have things I want to say, and I think they need to be said."

"I think that's fair," I said. My maturity level was at an all-time high. Being in a relationship really made me see things clearly, differently than I thought I would.

She scooted away and twisted her body so she could face me. "It was the worst two weeks of my life. I've been in relationships before, we both know that, but I was always so involved in things that I was able to move on quickly. I've been a mess. I found the perfect relationship with you."

I took her hands. She was shaking. I squeezed them for encouragement. I didn't want to interrupt her.

"Yes, I know there was a big thing between us, but I think now that it's out in the open, it will only strengthen us."

"I will try to tell you things, but just know that I've been private my entire life, so it's going to take me some time to get used to sharing," I said. She couldn't expect me to just blurt out everything all of the time. That was never going to be me.

"I do a pretty good job of giving you space when you need it," she said.

"I know and I agree. You've been extremely patient and sweet with my craziness and issues."

She touched my face. "You're not crazy. You just are working through life the best way you know how. I hope that I can help along the way." She kissed me swiftly, tentatively, as if I would reject her.

"That means more to me than you know," I said.

We spent the evening next to one another on the couch, talking about the simple things since so much was already said about the life-changing ones. There were a few sweet touches, soft kisses, but neither one of us wanted to rush back to where we were. I felt like a new person. My secret was out, and although it was liberating, I felt exposed.

"I missed you the past couple of weeks," she said.

She rubbed her fingers up and down mine in a soft, erotic way. Or maybe that was just the way I responded. Either way, it felt wonderful being touched by her again.

"How was the concert? I'm sorry I missed it."

"Oh, my God! I'm horrible." Hope sat up and stared at me. "Lily, your company is allowing us to convert one of their unused two-story buildings into the Leading Note. And we received an anonymous donation so we can set it up the way we want and maybe even get some new or slightly used furniture. I can't believe I didn't say anything sooner."

I smiled because Agnes kept my secret and Hope was very appreciative of everything that happened for the Leading Note. "You're not horrible. We just had a lot to talk about."

"Thank you for making this happen for us. I'm so happy. We'll spend the next few months getting it ready and then transfer the equipment and heavy instruments over there. It's close to where it was before and it's closer to your place. So, if you want, you can come by and play whenever you want. No pressure." She threw her arms around my neck and squeezed me. "You're fantastic."

"I really admire the center and what you've done with it. You have to understand that what you do for the children is completely different than anything I've ever known. I want this to be successful." Hope had such love in her life that I doubted she would ever understand what I went through growing up. "Now, tell me about the concert and leave nothing out."

"The kids performed wonderfully. We had a full house. Standing room only. Miles did a great job of bringing people in. I owe him," she said.

"More. I want details." I laughed at her stories of the mishaps and the surprises of the night. I decided I wasn't going to miss the next one, no matter what.

"It's late. I should probably go."

I didn't want her to leave, but I wasn't ready for her to stay either. We stood awkwardly at the door.

"Should I be concerned that we haven't seen Clio in hours?" she asked.

"I blame you if he's sprawled out somewhere in the back." I smiled.

"When do I get to see you again?" She moved in close and

gently placed her hands on my waist. She pulled me toward her when I didn't stop her.

"How about this weekend? Can we go to Blue Eden?"

Her eyes widened in surprise. "Of course we can." She kissed me good-bye with just enough passion to get me interested, and pulled away before we couldn't stop. "Thank you for letting me come over."

I closed the door behind her and leaned against it. My life had changed so much in just a matter of days, and for the first time since I was a small child, I felt completely at peace.

CHAPTER TWENTY-SEVEN

I've decided you should always wear black and your dresses should always be above your knee," I said.

Hope blushed and pulled me into her apartment. "You're just saying that. Black is so drab."

"Black is so sexy," I said, and kissed her softly. This time she stayed in my arms and deepened the kiss. It was a welcome surprise.

"I will do my best to keep my hands to myself, but I make no promises," Hope said. She stepped out of my embrace to look at me. "You look fantastic in jeans. Do a spin for me." I slowly turned and smiled when she made a growly sound deep in her throat. "These are new and I definitely approve."

I shrugged and stepped back, slightly embarrassed but empowered by her praise. "I do have a pair of nice jeans, but I think I might be underdressed compared to you."

Hope smiled. "You look great. And you're just my height."

I was wearing cute flats, but she was wearing strappy heels, so it evened us out. "Now you don't have to stand on your tiptoes to kiss me." I proved that by leaning forward and pressing my lips against hers. I held her close and kissed her again. She wasn't wearing a bra, and my body responded instantly. I wondered what else she wasn't wearing.

"I like this jeans and jacket look. If you get hot, you can just take this off." She pressed against me and slid the thin blazer past my shoulders. "I like this silky little number, too." I was wearing a sleeveless red blouse that hinted at the cleavage I was doing my best to show off, but not in a slutty way. There was only so much I could do without feeling uncomfortable. I didn't tell her that a sweet sales associate spent hours with me at Nordstrom to find the perfect outfit for tonight.

"I'm sure I'll get hot." I was already sweating, but it was more about Hope's outfit and less about the air-conditioned room. I hadn't seen Hope since dinner earlier this week, and even though I wanted to take it slow, I wanted her naked in my arms. I wanted to make her come for me, because of me, because of us. I was overwhelmed with emotions, but all good stuff. I was getting better at not freaking out.

"I'm sure you will, too." Hope's voice was dark and promising. I shivered and, for a split second, thought about staying and making love to her on the couch, but changed my mind. I wanted the world to see us together. I was ready to be a part of a couple, even if that put me in the spotlight from time to time.

The thickness of the heat and the heaviness of the noisy city pushed us into a cab. We wanted to walk for a bit, but we were both miserable after half a block. Even though my hair was piled up high on my head, a thin trickle of sweat formed at the back of my neck. Hope looked refreshed but assured me she felt the heat, too.

We both sighed when we opened the door to Blue Eden. The burst of cold air felt wonderful. There were a lot of people inside already and I immediately moved closer to Hope. She put her arm around my waist and leaned into me. "I reserved the same booth we were in last time."

"They let you reserve specific tables?"

"Miles does. Especially since it's not front and center. Nobody cares about a side booth near the back." She offered me the wall of the booth and slid in beside me. A waitress buzzed over to us immediately to get our drinks. Hope ordered us gin and tonics with extra limes. I was beginning to appreciate the smoothness of alcohol.

"Tell me about the performers tonight." The house band was warming up the crowd and playing low enough to allow patrons to chat and drink. Local favorite Brooklyn Trio was next, followed by Bryan King and his entire band of twelve musicians. I hoped to be gone by then.

"I love Brooklyn Trio because they are fun and really play to the crowd. Once you see them, you'll understand why I like them so much. Have you heard of Bryan King?" Hope asked.

I shook my head. I listened to the oldies. It wasn't that I was opposed to modern jazz, I just hadn't wanted to open myself up to new music. I knew Hope would help me hear music the way it was supposed to be heard—with joy and excitement, not fear and trepidation. "Pretend I know nothing about jazz. What can I expect from him?"

She told me Bryan King's life story, but halfway though, my thoughts turned and I couldn't have cared less about him. I couldn't stop staring at Hope's full lips. I remembered them all over my body, kissing me everywhere.

"Lily? Where'd you go?" I shook my head briefly, trying to shake off my thoughts, but I was in too deep. I missed her. I missed her mouth, her warmth, and our intimacy. I missed sex. I missed holding her and the feeling of letting go in her arms.

"How long do we have to stay?"

"We can leave right now if it's too much for you." She reached out and touched my arm supportively.

"It's not too much for me. It just hit me how much I've missed us." Heat crept up my neck and landed in my cheeks. It was obvious where my thoughts were and I lowered my eyes. I didn't know how to ask for intimacy. I wasn't sure how to tell her what I wanted.

"Let's go." She knew. Hope waited for me to slide out of the booth before she reached for my hand. She pressed against me, and just as we were making our way out of the bar, Miles stepped in front of us.

"Where are you two going? You just got here like twenty minutes ago." He kissed Hope's cheek and reached for my hand. "And we missed you at the concert, Lily. Your girl put on quite the show."

"I heard and I'm sorry I missed it. It sounded like a great time. I won't miss the next one." I almost rolled my eyes when he kept the conversation going.

"And I heard Leading Note is moving. That's great news. Let me know if you need help moving. Me and the guys would love to help out."

"Oh, I'll definitely hold you to that." Hope turned to me and said, "Miles helped move us into our current building."

Hope smiled at him and wrapped her arm around my waist. Her fingertips slipped under the blazer and blouse to caress my bare skin. She was seducing me in front of Miles, and I was both embarrassed and incredibly turned on.

"I have plenty of experience moving pianos. You already know this. I'll let the guys know to be on call."

"Thank you again, and I'm sorry we have to leave so suddenly, but we'll be back another time." Hope kissed his cheek and we finally made our way out of the bar.

The heat hadn't eased up at all. I slipped off my jacket and folded it over my arm as we waited for a cab. In thirty seconds, we were in an air-conditioned cab that reeked of overripe bananas and cheap cologne. A faint cigar smell lingered even though there were No Smoking stickers everywhere. Hope gave the driver her address and we sat back and waited in silence. I was afraid to even touch her for fear that I wouldn't be able to stop.

I threw money at the driver and scooted out of the cab. Did I just give him a forty-dollar tip on a ten-dollar ride? Hope reached her hand out to me and I took it. We quickly made our way up the stairs to her apartment. I put both hands, palms flat, against the door on either side of her as I waited for her to find her keys. I pressed into her from behind and moaned when she leaned her head back on my shoulder and pushed back into me.

"What's taking so long?" I growled in her ear before sucking her earlobe into my mouth and gently biting down. She moaned again, although this time it sounded more passionate, more animalistic.

"You're distracting me," she breathed. Her hand shook when she finally got the key in the slot and unlocked the door. She pushed the door open and we both stumbled inside. She kept walking and dropped clothes in her wake. "Don't forget to lock the door."

I fumbled to get the door closed. By the time I had done it, Hope had disappeared into her bedroom. I followed her. She was waiting for me by the bed, fully naked and submissive. I kicked off my jeans and slipped out of the thin blouse on my way to her. She crawled on the bed and knelt on the edge when I approached.

"You still have too many clothes on." She hooked her thumbs in my panties and slid them down my thighs until they dropped to my ankles. I reached back and unclasped my bra. She eagerly pulled it off and tossed it somewhere behind me.

"I missed you," I said.

She pulled me into her and fell back on the bed, taking me with her in the process. I nestled my hips between her legs.

We both moaned at the contact. "I've missed you, too." She captured my mouth in a heart-pounding, passionate kiss.

We fell into the rhythm that lovers do, but this time, it felt different. We were different. The secret that had wedged itself between our hearts was gone, and I could fully give myself to Hope. I touched her everywhere, memorizing her every curve, soft and sharp. She wound her hands in my hair as I journeyed down her body, my lips pressing a path until I reached her wet folds. I spread her apart and tasted her. Her hands held my head steady where she wanted my mouth. I slid two fingers inside her, in and out slowly until she pleaded with me to go faster and harder.

Hope writhing in my arms, begging me to fuck her was so empowering. She wanted me to take charge. I sucked her clit into my mouth and moved my hand as fast as I could. In a matter of seconds, her hips bucked against me. She cried out and grabbed my shoulders as she rode out her orgasm. I felt her pulsate around my fingers, drenching them with her essence that I eagerly lapped up. Her clit, swollen and smooth, was too sensitive, so I moved away from it but kept my fingers deep inside her. I could stay like this forever—my head on her thigh, her hands stroking my hair, both of us hidden from the rest of the world.

"I love you, Lily."

I wasn't sure she said it. I held my breath and waited. Maybe she would say it again. And again.

"I love you. I know we have a long way to go, but I needed you to know." She twirled my hair around her fingers. "I don't expect you to say anything to me. Just know."

I looked up at her. My heart hammered inside my chest, threatening to spill out between us. When was the last time I said the word "love"? Probably to Clio. When was the last time I said it to another person? I told my parents and grandparents that I loved them, but this was a different kind of emotion. This was deeper, more raw, and originated from somewhere I couldn't identify. My body hummed whenever she was near. I felt alive with her. For the first time, I felt something real.

"I…" I cleared my voice and started again. "I love you, too." My voice sounded scratchy and dry. I was bad at this, but I needed her to know I felt the same way.

Her fingers tightened in my hair. "You don't have to say it back."

I scooted up to face her. She caressed my cheek. "I'm serious. I love you, Hope D'Marco. I knew it when we had breakfast at the little restaurant in my neighborhood."

Her face broke out into the most amazing smile I'd ever seen. She wrapped her arms around my neck and kissed me hard. "I fell in love with you that time you sat under the window at Leading Note and judged me."

I tickled her until she gasped for breath. "I wasn't judging you." She raised her eyebrow at me. "Okay, I was, but it was all for a good cause."

"A good cause?" She kissed me. "Good?"

"A great cause. A wonderful cause." I leaned down and kissed her again.

"I appreciate and respect all your advice. Truly." She placed her hand on my heart. "I'm in love with my own heroine. I love you and who you are today, and I love the musician inside you. I can't believe how lucky I am." She flipped me and trailed her lips over my body. "Tell me what you hear."

"Now?" I gasped when her teeth grazed my nipple. I felt her nod against my chest. "I hear my heartbeat." I paused when she swirled her tongue over to my other breast.

"What else?" Her voice was more of a purr.

I closed my eyes again. "I can hear the blood rushing in my body. I can hear you breathing."

She crawled up my body and I smiled when I felt her lips barely brush mine. She whispered, "What else?"

"I hear love. Your sweet words. I'll never get tired of hearing it. Tell me every day." I was breathless from wanting her touch and slightly frustrated that she wasn't complying.

"Tell me what you want," she said against my mouth.

"I want you."

"You have me. What do you want?" she asked again.

"I want you to make love to me. Right now. I'm desperate for you." I was rewarded with a passionate kiss and the full weight of her body on top of mine. I moved against her, anxious for friction. I cupped her ass and pushed into her, wiggling my hips in repetitive motion against her.

Hope slid her hand between us and slipped inside me. We moved together, our own music, our own rhythm. In that moment, right before I came in her arms, I knew this was meant to be. I knew we were destined to be together. She whispered how happy she was, but what I felt was far greater than happiness. I felt free, released from my own prison. I knew I had a lot to learn about life and love, but I knew we were going to survive. I had peace. I had a purpose. Most of all, and most importantly, I had Hope.

Epilogue

W hat are you doing with that?" Hope nodded at the marker I had in my hand. She was lying in bed, her body curved around a book she was reading, her forgotten coffee cup on the nightstand beside her. My stealthy yet extremely exaggerated slip into the room had gotten her attention. "You'll never be James Bond."

"Maybe I could be Jane Bond. Don't be sexist, love." I crept over to her like the Grinch who stole Christmas.

"Seriously, what are you going to do?" She finally closed the book and watched me warily as I approached the bed.

"Stretch your legs out," I said.

She obliged. "I'm definitely intrigued, but a marker? Couldn't we try something a little bigger?" She laughed when I blushed and crawled on the bed beside her.

"Since our piano won't be here for another two hours, I thought I'd get some practice time in now." Hope had moved in three months ago. And after encouragement and a lot more therapy, I bought a grand piano. We got rid of the dining room table and planned to put the Mason & Hamlin in its spot so it overlooked the city. I was unsure of the acoustics in the condo, but Hope told me to quit being a snob and everything would be okay. I pulled the sheet off her hip and uncapped the black marker. I made two parallel lines, six inches apart, from her hip to her knee. I drew lines connecting the two and watched her smile out of the corner of my eye.

"Washable," I whispered and showed her the marker. I sparsely colored in ten black keys and leaned back to admire my work. The makeshift keyboard on her leg was clever, and I smiled at my creation.

She nodded her approval as well.

"Okay, so I have two octaves here. What do you want me to play?"

Hope flopped back against the pillow, careful to not move her leg. "Play me one of your encores. Something you loved to play."

I pointed down. "I'm limited here."

"Then play what you can."

"Okay, tell me what you hear." I silently played "Chopsticks." She laughed at me and brushed my hands away. I gave her a serious nod and played a song that was easy to play given my restricted space.

"I'm going to go with Mozart."

"You're really bad at this." I pressed harder so she would feel the keys as I played them. Even watching me she struggled.

"I just can't figure it out. Give me a hint."

I cleared my throat and hummed a few bars.

"You're playing Pink!" Her jaw fell open in surprise. "When did you learn Pink?"

I shrugged like it wasn't a big deal, but I saw the delight in her expression. "You had the music somewhere on a bookshelf and I just studied it." We both knew I spent about thirty seconds looking at it and memorized it.

"That's so wonderful. I can't wait to hear you play it later tonight."

I could only have an audience of one, but it was a big step for me. Hope never bothered me when I wanted to play or asked that I play her something. She always left the decision up to me.

"I guess you probably should get ready, huh?" I pointed down to her leg. "That should wash right off in the shower. If it doesn't, call me."

"It's not like anyone is going to see my bare leg even if it doesn't wash off." Hope was going to the Leading Note on her day off only because another shipment of instruments was going to be delivered. "I plan on bundling up. I hate winter, but that's Chicago for you." She sighed and struggled to push herself into a sitting position. "I don't want to leave you, but I'm kind of excited to see what arrives today."

I'd reached out to several conductors and symphonies I'd worked with in the past and asked them to donate any instruments they no longer used. Most of them didn't believe it was me because I had been away for so long, but with a few gentle reminders of tantrums I'd thrown, or mistakes I made or ones they made, they all came around. Word spread fast and people were trying to reach me to do concerts or interviews, but I turned them all down. My life had changed. I had a different goal. I loved music and would forever, but I loved what Hope was doing more and the reasons behind her dreams. The response I received from the people I reached out to was overwhelming. Hope was working with other foundations and schools in and around the Chicago area to share all of the instruments that were generously donated. That only made the Leading Note all the more popular. Gene's daughter-in-law did a fantastic cover story to generate interest, and her follow-up piece was just as successful. The Leading Note was growing. Hope had hired four more instructors and three office personnel just to keep up.

"Go get ready. I'll make you a fresh coffee to go." I jumped up and reached out for her hand to help her up.

She groaned playfully and pulled me back on the bed instead. "What if I want to stay here and play with you all day?"

"I can go instead and you can wait for the piano," I said.

She groaned again. "I wish we could do both together."

I leaned down and kissed her nose. "I know, but tonight is going to be special. So, the sooner you get to work and do a quick inventory, the sooner you can come home and meet our new baby."

Hope hid her surprise well when I said we should go check out pianos a few weeks ago. We rarely used the dining room, and it was too nice a space to go to waste. We didn't entertain people, and if we wanted a nice meal, we could eat at the kitchen bar.

"I can't wait. Okay, I'm going." She raced to the bathroom to get ready. I handed her a travel mug of hot coffee on her way out the door. She stopped and kissed me firmly on the mouth. "I love you. I can't wait to meet our new addition."

❖

She was beautiful. Sleek, black, and very quiet. The professional who accompanied the movers tuned it perfectly. He asked if I would like to play it while he was still there, but I trusted his ear and declined. He polished a few smudges out until he was completely satisfied the piano was perfect.

"I just wanted you to know that I've always enjoyed your music, and I hope this piano brings you happiness again. It's the perfect comeback instrument." He nodded as if he understood and accepted my struggles, put on his hat and coat, and walked out the door. I should have been creeped out that he knew who

I was, but I was surprisingly calm and my attention was solely on the piano. It was just me and her. And Clio, who jumped on the windowsill and looked at it from across the room.

"The first scratches I see on her from you, I swear I will put you in mittens. Then you'll wish you were still outside." He yawned, knowing full well I would never follow through on my threats. I pulled out the bench and sat on the edge, eager, nervous, and excited. I flipped up the fallboard and stared at the eighty-eight keys. I missed them. I ran my fingers gently across the tops, my touch as light as a caress. I pushed down on the pedals to get a feel for their stiffness. I sat up a little taller, waited for the adrenaline to reach my fingers, and hit the keys. I played anything and everything my heart wanted. I was still good. I wasn't great like before and I stumbled over a few notes when my fingers weren't fast enough for my brain, but I still had it. I smiled. I wasn't afraid. I slid back on the bench and waited to see what reaction I would have. My hands shook a little bit, but that was probably because I lacked the stamina I once had.

"Please keep playing."

I hadn't heard Hope come in. I honestly had no idea how much time had passed since they delivered the piano.

"What time is it?"

She flipped her wrist up. "Four fifteen." She placed her coat on the rack and wrapped her scarf over the collar. "She's beautiful, Lily. She looks perfect in here." She walked over to me and put her arms around my neck. "What do you think?"

I loved the feel of her warm lips against my temple. She made me feel safe.

"Have a seat and find out." I slid over to give her room, but she waved me off and sat on the couch.

"If you still feel like playing, I'd love to hear you."

My adrenaline spiked again. She sent me a suggestive

look. I turned back around and placed my fingers on the keys. Hope had once told me that the piano was sad, so I decided to change her mind. I played "Waltz of the Flowers" by Tchaikovsky because it was one of my favorites and I loved the challenge of it. I'd started playing it when I first sat down, but everything had come rushing back to me and I couldn't stay focused long enough to complete one song. I started with one song that had a bar or note that reminded me of another song, so I slipped from composer to composer, never completing an entire piece, until now. I wanted this to be perfect. Hope told me I was her favorite, even when she was a little girl. That was so empowering, and I wanted nothing more than to make her happy, so I played it from the heart and I played it perfectly. When I was done, I turned back around to find Hope in tears. This time I smiled.

"Did you like it?" I stood up and walked over to the couch. She reached for me and pulled me down next to her. I handed her a box of tissues, which she gratefully accepted.

"Just so you know, I'm always going to cry when you play," she said.

"But they are the good tears. Happy tears."

"They are love tears," she said.

"There is no such thing." I kissed her softly.

"You know that there is." She straddled my lap, my new favorite place for her to be. I held her hips and let her finish her thought. My plan was to flip her after she explained herself. "It's all this love I feel for you. I can't deal with it. I don't know how to process it, so I cry." She leaned down and kissed me softly. "Remember the first time we made love?"

I leaned back and groaned. "I was an amateur."

She poked my side until I laughed. "I believe you were a beginner. And I believe we kissed one another's tears away."

"I never cry. I don't know what you're talking about," I said. Lies.

She held my face in her hands. "I love you, Lily Croft, and from here on out, I will only cry happy tears around you for all of the right reasons, even during sex." Her confession made me want to cry.

"I love you, too, Hope D'Marco. And we both know I cry at everything, especially during sex. You're responsible for all the good in my life. Especially her." I pointed behind her at the piano.

"Are you already done playing?"

"It's your turn." I squeezed her hips and slid her off my lap. Instead of heading to the piano, she sat back down on the couch.

"Hearing you play is my dream come true. If you're in a good place, I'd like to hear a little more."

I headed back to the piano. I felt sure and confident. There was nothing to conquer anymore. I was never going to be Jillian Crest again, but I could be Lily Croft with an audience of one. I'd made peace with that. I looked at Hope. "Is there anything in particular that you want me to play?"

Her face broke into the biggest smile that lit up my heart. "Whatever you want, babe. I'm here to love you and support you. Right now, I just want to sit back and listen."

About the Author

Kris Bryant was born in Tacoma, WA, but has lived all over the world and now considers Kansas City her home. She received her BA in English from the University of Missouri and spends a lot of her time buried in books. She enjoys hiking, photography, and spending time with her family and her dog, Molly.

Her first novel, *Jolt*, was a Lambda Literary Finalist and Rainbow Awards Honorable Mention. Her second book, *Whirlwind Romance*, was a Rainbow Runner-up for Contemporary Romance. *Taste* was also a Rainbow Awards Honorable Mention for Contemporary Romance. *Forget Me Not* was selected by the American Library Association's 2018 Over the Rainbow book list and was a Golden Crown Finalist for Contemporary Romance.

Books Available From Bold Strokes Books

A Chapter on Love by Laney Webber. When Jannika and Lee reunite, their instant connection feels like a gift, but neither is ready for a second chance at love. Will they finally get on the same page when it comes to love? (978-1-163555-366-6)

Drawing Down the Mist by Sheri Lewis Wohl. Everyone thinks Grand Duchess Maria Romanova died in 1918. They were almost right. (978-1-163555-341-3)

Listen by Kris Bryant. Lily Croft is inexplicably drawn to Hope D'Marco, but will she have the courage to confront the consequences of her past and present colliding? (978-1-163555-318-5)

Perfect Partners by Maggie Cummings. Elite police dog trainer Sara Wright has no intention of falling in love with a coworker until Isabel Marquez arrives at Homeland Security's Northeast Regional Training facility, and Sara's good intentions start to falter. (978-1-163555-363-5)

Shut Up and Kiss Me by Julie Cannon. What better way to spend two weeks of hell in paradise than in the company of a hot, sexy woman? (978-1-163555-343-7)

Spencer's Cove by Missouri Vaun. When Foster Owen and Abigail Spencer meet, they uncover a story of lives adrift, loves lost, and true love found. (978-1-163555-171-6)

Unexpected Lightning by Cass Sellars. Lightning strikes once more when Sydney and Parker fight a dangerous stranger who threatens the peace they both desperately want. (978-1-163555-276-8)

Without Pretense by TJ Thomas. After living for decades hiding from the truth, can Ava learn to trust Bianca with her secrets and her heart? (978-1-163555-173-0)

Emily's Art and Soul by Joy Argento. When Emily meets Andi Marino she thinks she's found a new best friend, but Emily doesn't know that Andi is fast falling in love with her. Caught up in exploring her sexuality, will Emily see the only woman she needs is right in front of her? (978-1-163555-355-0)

Escape to Pleasure: Lesbian Travel Erotica, edited by Sandy Lowe and Victoria Villaseñor. Join these award-winning authors as they explore the sensual side of erotic lesbian travel. (978-1-163555-339-0)

Music City Dreamers by Robyn Nyx. Music can bring lovers together. In Music City, it can tear them apart. (978-1-163555-207-2)

Ordinary is Perfect by D. Jackson Leigh. Atlanta marketing superstar Autumn Swan's life derails when she inherits a country home, a child, and a very interesting neighbor. (978-1-163555-280-5)

Royal Court by Jenny Frame. When royal dresser Holly Weaver's passionate personality begins to melt Royal Marine Captain Quincy's icy heart, will Holly be ready for what she exposes beneath? (978-1-163555-290-4)

Strings Attached by Holly Stratimore. Rock star Nikki Razer always gets what she wants, but when she falls for Drew McNally, a music teacher who won't date celebrities, can she convince Drew she's worth the risk? (978-1-163555-347-5)

The Ashford Place by Jean Copeland. When Isabelle Ashford inherits an old house in small-town Connecticut, family secrets, a shocking discovery, and an unexpected romance complicate her plan for a fast profit and a temporary stay. (978-1-163555-316-1)

Treason by Gun Brooke. Zoem Malderyn's existence is a deadly threat to everyone on Gemocon, and Commander Neenja KahSandra must find a way to save the woman she loves from having to make the ultimate sacrifice. (978-1-163555-244-7)

A Wish Upon a Star by Jeannie Levig. Erica Cooper has learned to depend on only herself, but when her new neighbor, Leslie Raymond, befriends Erica's special needs daughter, the walls protecting Erica's heart threaten to crumble. (978-1-163555-274-4)

Answering the Call by Ali Vali. Detective Sept Savoie returns to the streets of New Orleans, as do the dead bodies from ritualistic killings, and she does everything in her power to bring their killers to justice while trying to keep her partner, Keegan Blanchard, safe. (978-1-163555-050-4)